I0701629

Loaded for Bear

Adventures and Misadventures
from the Appalachians to the Chesapeake

Loaded for Bear
By George Miller

Copyright 2024
By George Miller
All Rights Reserved

Editor
Sandra Olivetti Martin
New Bay Books
Fairhaven, Maryland
NewBayBooks@gmail.com

Cover Photo:
"Baseball Mitt" by William Lambrecht

Cover and interior design by Suzanne Shelden
Shelden Studios
Prince Frederick, Maryland
sheldenstudios@comcast.net

A Note on Type:
Cover and section heads and text
are set in Adobe Jenson Pro.
Body text is set in Garamond Premier Pro.

Library of Congress
Cataloging-in-Publication Data

979-8-9882998-2-0

Printed in the United States of America
First Edition

Table of Contents

The narrator at peace in the garden
before the "misadventures" to follow.

—painting by June Kirkpatrick Ciancio

Introduction

For thirty years I rode the Commuter Rail from Western Maryland into the District of Columbia. Many of the stories in this collection were conceived on the train. The morning ride into the city offered uninterrupted quiet to transform sentence fragments scribbled on scraps of paper into coherent paragraphs. Some notes I consolidated into stories. Others lay dormant for years in a shoebox in the back of my bedroom closet. The afternoon ride home provided an incubator, the raw materials for the next round of scribblings: characters, emotions, affairs, tragedies, drunken escapades, temptations— no imagination necessary—just listen. Today, when I find myself out of ideas, I return to the shoebox in the back of my closet to refresh my memory.

My fellow passengers boarded the train at Union Station at the end of the workday, some ready to unwind, some to party, more than a few with a briefcase in one hand, a six pack in the other, and stories to share. Most trains were configured with a party car at one end, the quiet car at the other, and gradations in-between. The party car was the mother load of inspiration. A half-pint of Sierra Nevada Pale Ale was sufficient to coax a good story from most travelers. Among these are "Cousins," "Mom Takes a Fall," "Trifecta," "A Road Trip" and yet another bear story, "Rules for Repelling a Bear."

I've lived most of my life in Maryland, a crescent from Cumberland in the west, Montgomery County in the middle, and Chesapeake Beach in the southeast. I can credit my own personal experience for "Breech Birth," "Green Card," and

"Loaded for Bear." Two involuntary years in the army in the late 1960s provided inspiration for "The Oxymoron and the Baltimorean" and "Psych Wing."

I included "Shotgun Wedding," "Get Out of Jail Free," and "A Pal's Last Need" to make my life sound more interesting than it really was. There is an element of truth in all stories, although, as the fictitious editor at the end of "Breech Birth" concludes, "Nobody will believe that."

I hope you find my stories authentic and worthy of your time. They're as real as it gets these days. As the fictitious narrator at the beginning of "Breech Birth" observes, "It's a niche market, not as lame as you might think." Thank you for visiting my niche.

Loaded for Bear

Adventures and Misadventures
from the Appalachians to the Chesapeake

By George Miller

Loaded for Bear

Thirteen-year-old boys don't process all five senses at the same time. We left-brained juveniles filter out extraneous stimulation unrelated to the task at hand. During the predawn hours of January 30, 1960, the task at hand was a cowhide catcher's mitt, temporarily residing in the display window of the Centre Street Sports Store.

In my world, we play by the hand we're dealt. I was dealt a dying grandfather who hoped to live to see the Pittsburgh Pirates win a World Series; my father, a Presbyterian minister, who believed all rewards are earned and not given; and a newspaper route at the corner of Greene and Lee streets in the mountain town of Cumberland, Maryland. I sold the *Times-News* to South End workers on their way to jobs in the factories along the Potomac River. Being thirteen years old without my own dream, I was subsumed by my grandfather's. I had a lifetime ahead of me. He had only a stroke-ridden eightieth year at best. I was all in on the Pirates.

I passed the sports store window several times a week, always anxious when I approached, fretting whether my mitt was still available. My grandfather agreed to pay half if I earned an equal share from my paper route. Once when the shopkeeper was busy selling football paraphernalia, I scooted the glove behind a Johnny Unitas football jersey where it was less likely to be noticed. I was focused, anticipating my fist smacking into the tobacco-tanned leather, the collision of ball and mitt when I took the field.

At 5:30 a.m. on any weekday, I parked my bicycle outside the print shop on Mechanic Street, located my stack of papers on the loading dock, snipped the binding cord with my wire cutters, divided the papers between two saddle bags, and hand-wheeled my bicycle across the Baltimore Street Bridge west on Greene Street. I positioned myself on the northeast corner at the traffic light where I had a clear view of cars traveling west. My corner at Greene and Lee was filled with sensory stimulation, all unrelated to my catcher's mitt: the glare of approaching headlamps, locomotives belching steam into the mist at the B&O rail yard, the stench of rubber molds at the Kelly Springfield Tire plant, the rumble of Wills Creek through the storm channel into the river, the wail of the foghorn at Celanese Fibers signaling the shift change. I filtered out the ice crystals on my eye lashes, the cold steel of the wire cutters, the sharp recoil of the binding wire, the heft of newspapers swinging left and right over my rear tire, and the acrid odor of newsprint penetrating my nostrils. Several times a year, an accident at Allegany Ballistics rattled the town with an explosion that penetrated my senses before my left brain could activate an operative filter.

My concentration focused on the clank of nickels dropping into my coin dispenser. I recognized the exact harmonic when the nickels' stack registered $2.50, fifty nickels for fifty newspapers. Only then did I allow the waft of deep-fried dough from Capprielli's Bakery across the way to penetrate my nostrils. At that threshold I entitled myself to a raspberry jelly-filled doughnut on my way home.

Standing on the curb, staring at the approaching headlamps, I had only a few seconds to prepare my sales pitch. It wasn't easy coaxing a nickel out of blue-collar workers with their Popeye forearms. Over time I learned to work the crowd. My ace in the hole was my imitation of a Kelly Belly, the trademark of Kelly-Springfield workers who treated themselves to a bucket of Old German beer and a bottomless bag of unshelled peanuts at the Jägermeister after work. Car after car slowed to marvel at the distended belly protruding from my bony torso.

"Hey, look at that Kelly Belly. The kid has potential. Somebody give him a nickel."

Midway through my shift, the 6:10 Western Maryland freight train blocked the Baltimore Street crossing, offering me a few minutes to fine tune my marketing strategy. An obvious catch was the newspaper crime report. My favorites were:

- Police search for man who robbed Mason's Jug Store on Greene Street with a rubber knife late Tuesday.

- A city man, wanted for robbing an elderly woman in her West End home Wednesday evening, is also a suspect in a home evasion in Flintstone. Police suspect insider involvement.

- And this news break: West Virginia resident arrested Thursday for smoking dope in western Maryland welfare line.

From my corner, I had a clear view of cars driving from the Algonquian Hotel into the parking lot of Wagner and Sons Funeral Home. These were typically former residents who returned to Cumberland from enclaves across southern Pennsylvania to bury their grannies. I played a game of matching headlines in my newspapers with the arriving vehicles of the bereaved:

- Second Degree Mason dies in hunting accident (Packard Roadster).

- Elder at Bear Creek Church of the Brethren finds eternal rest (Nash Rambler).

- Decorated veteran honored at VFW memorial service (Willys Jeep).

- Pittsburgh Plate Glass foreman dies in tragic accident on factory floor (Pontiac Bonneville).

Perhaps the deceased relative may have been in an obituary; only cost a nickel to find out. My father lectured me on the difference between a death notice and an obituary. On the street we made no such distinction, a mention was a mention, a nickel was a nickel, a fabrication was a fabrication.

Such was my frame of mind on January 30, 1960, at 6:45 a.m., only one paper in my satchel, $2.45 in my coin dispenser, the scent of fresh doughnuts drifting across the train tracks from the bakery. As I tallied my take for the day, I noticed a Cadillac with Pennsylvania license plates easing along the street in my direction, the same car I'd spotted in the Algonquian Hotel parking lot on my way from the print shop, definitely a good candidate for my final customer and a big fat tip.

I considered my sales pitch, a moot point since the Caddy pulled into the circular drive in front of the funeral home and rolled to a stop under the light of the awning. Its interior lights flashed on and off several times. Two long-legged men emerged from the front seat and spread a map across the hood. As they studied the map, the back doors swung open, not just swung open, but swung open on rear hinges, suicide doors in the vernacular. Two other men emerged from the back and joined the two studying the map.

My father objected to the loaded term suicide doors since he was in the emotional support business. He preferred to call them coach doors, but not until after a long-winded digression into nineteenth century horse-drawn carriages, annotated with Marcel Proust sensations and details. My uncluttered thirteen-year-old brain filtered out any mention of Marcel Proust.

All four men struggled to hold the map in place. Gradually, slowly, their focus turned to me, in plain view under the mercury streetlamp. My thoughts oscillated between the danger posed by out-of-town strangers and a big fat tip on my final sale. I instinctively covered my coin dispenser with my jacket, mistakenly supposing that grown men who could afford a Cadillac might rob a paperboy for $2.45 and steal his bicycle.

They returned to their car, eased left on Greene Street, and slowed to a stop at my corner, giving me a closer look through the tinted windows. Skull-and-crossbones pennants flapping in the wind from the radio antenna jacked up my anxiety level.

One of the men emerged from the left rear door, adjusting the visor on his baseball cap as he approached. I lowered my hand to protect my coin dispenser. Speaking with a broad sweep of his arms, he asked, "Young man, you from around here?"

He definitely violated my space since my comfort zone ballooned out five or six feet. My inner thirteen-year-old imagined kidnappers, or worse yet, child molesters. My mother's repeated warnings rose to the fore. "Don't tell strangers where you live."

Her warning came too late. "Yeah, my parents live up the hill on McGregor."

The driver's power window buzzed down. "Buddy, do you know who I am?"

I turned to answer, stalling for time. "Sure I do. Give me a minute."

"I'll give you a hint, third base for the Dodgers in the 1955 World Series."

Not much help since I was eight years old in 1955. The other man in the back seat chimed in. "Playing behind Jackie Robinson."

I knew who Jackie Robinson was. Mine was a progressive family quite familiar with the first black man to break the color barrier in major league white baseball. My father covered that one during one of his breakfast table lectures on racial tolerance.

I leaned forward for a closer look, but the man in the passenger seat interrupted, changing the subject. "Hey, kid, do you know what kind of car this is?"

I sensed an opportunity to demonstrate my knowledge of late 1950s' luxury automobiles. "Who doesn't? A Cadillac Eldo..."

Before I could finish, he answered his own question. "Close, but not just any Eldorado, a 1957 Eldorado Brougham, brushed stainless-steel roof, suicide doors, power windows, forged aluminum wheels, leather trim."

My tip radar was activated. I was thinking maybe a quarter or even fifty cents.

The man with the baseball hat reentered my comfort zone, "Maybe you can help us out. We need to find Oakland."

Before I could answer, the driver poked his head out the window and offered another hint. "Think 1957 All Star Team for the National League."

I played along. "Who doesn't?"

He extended his hand from the window, "Don Hoak, glad to meet you."

The man in the passenger seat asked. "How about me, kid? Ever seen me before?"

The man in the backseat answered that question, "Shut up, Harv, nobody cares about pitchers."

He pointed to my saddle bags, "What you selling there?"

"*Cumberland Times-News*, five cents."

"Is there a hunting section?"

"Last page of sports."

The driver took charge, "Maz, give the kid a nickel."

The man in the baseball hat pressed a coin into my palm. I handed him the newspaper. He turned to the man in the backseat. "Smoky, hand me a pen. This kid will bring us luck."

They passed the newspaper around, each of them signing it. The driver handed the paper back to me. "Here, this will pay for your college education, signed by starters for the Pittsburgh Pirates."

Four signatures emerged under the streetlight: Smoky Burgess, Don Hoak, Bill Mazeroski, Harvey Haddix. This was the 1950s. I was thirteen, the age when I bought anything I was told, unless someone might suppose I was gullible enough to believe that a carload of major league baseball players miraculously appeared on my corner at 6:45 a.m. My brain required a few minutes to accommodate my eyes. I recognized the names and faces from my baseball card collection but never imagined seeing them in person.

"Hey, kid, how do we get to Oakland? There's a bear with my name on it prowling the hills," Mazeroski asked as he reached into the car, pulled out a double-barreled shotgun off the rack in the rear window, flipped open the breech, and shoved two buckshot cartridges into the chamber.

I didn't mean to offend these fellas, but the words slipped out. "My dad says never hunt bear with buckshot. It just makes them mad."

"We'll worry about that when we get to Oakland, Oakland, West BY GOD Virginia," as you people say.

My mouth continued on its own offensive streak. I'd attended nature camp in Garrett County. Precision is important. "Oakland is in Maryland."

"Okay, Oakland BY GOD Maryland. How do we get there? We're supposed to meet up with a grizzly backwoods guide."

I visualized a bearded mountaineer strolling through the forest with a magic marker writing names on bears. Fortunately, I had my Boy Scout merit badge in Pathfinding. "On the other side of Haystack Mountain, catch route 40 west toward Frostburg, before dropping down to Oakland."

Burgess interrupted with a question. "Young man, are you a baseball player?"

"Some, little league."

"What position?"

"Switching to catcher. Coach thinks I've got the right stance. I'm saving up for a mitt at Centre Street Sports."

"Somebody give the kid a tip. Let's get him that glove."

Hoak handed me a five-dollar bill and eased the Caddy out into traffic. Halfway through the intersection, he stopped and backed up to my corner. The rear window powered down. A hand reached out and handed me a catcher's mitt. "You'll do great behind the plate. Your coach is right about your stance. Don't give up."

I read the signature on the glove: Smoky Burgess. I turned to thank him, but the Cadillac disappeared through the industrial fog toward Garrett County to hunt bear with buckshot.

The stainless-steel roof glistened in the mercury streetlamp. I stood on the curb with the catcher's mitt cradled in my arms, stroking the leather to assure myself the moment was real. Instinctively I slipped the mitt under my lapel, sure that someone out for a morning stroll in the Greene Street fog might recognize my treasure and snatch it from my arms. Too dizzy from the excitement, I walked my bicycle across the tracks to Capprielli's Bakery before heading home to McGregor Street with $2.75 in my coin dispenser, a five-dollar bill in my pocket, a jelly doughnut, and a Smoky Burgess catcher's mitt. I was in heaven.

Decades later, my Uncle Howard and I visited the Antiques Roadshow in Pittsburgh for a definitive authentication. The catcher's mitt might bring $125 due to its excellent condition. The newspaper the appraiser lowballed at $75 even though it was autographed by four Pittsburgh starters because of the faded newsprint and torn corners. However, he appraised the two together at a premium since the newspaper documented the exact date of the exchange, not enough for a college education, but enough for bragging rights.

I spent my little league career sitting on the bench. I paid for my own college education and kept the newspaper and the glove in a trunk in my attic.

POSTSCRIPT

On January 30, 1959, a year before my predawn encounter at Greene and Lee streets, the Pittsburgh Pirates had traded

Whammy Douglas, Jim Pendleton, Frank Thomas, and John Powers to the Cincinnati Reds for Smoky Burgess, Harvey Haddix and Don Hoak. We didn't learn of the trade for several days until Granddad's Sunday edition of the *Pittsburgh Press* arrived in the mail.

The old man had moved in with us after he'd suffered the first of several debilitating strokes. He had been, and I quote, "kidnapped from my home in Pittsburgh by my bossy daughter when I'm perfectly able to care for myself."

For emphasis he'd added, "I practiced medicine for fifty-five years, treated worse strokes than this."

His assessment wasn't correct. His life had been a mess. He'd hardly been able to turn the pages in the newspaper, barely tamp his cigar ashes onto his dessert plate. After a second stroke, his speech had descended into monosyllabic gibberish. When he'd speak, he'd see his words float before his eyes, words that wouldn't stream down compromised neurons to his lips. He and I had developed a sign language to supplement his deteriorating vocalization: right swoop for turn the page, wipe drool from lip for excitement, thumb suck for sneak me a shot of whiskey. I'd become a one-boy translation service.

When I'd open the newspaper to the sports page, Granddad had grabbed my wrist with his gnarled hand and motioned for me to read aloud. His grip had tightened as I read the names, "Burgess, Haddix, Hoak,"

His eyes and my lips had synced onto a single word, Smoky, the puff of smoke when the bat hits the ball, when the pitch smacks into the catcher's mitt. That day we added a new symbol to our homegrown sign language: cigar quiver for Smoky Burgess. Even today when I feel despondent, I sign myself through any issues with a conversation only Granddad and I understand. I see a single word drift before my eyes, a quiver in my fingers, colloid cigar smoke shimmering up to the ceiling. I see Smoky, the catcher for the Pirates in the late 1950s, the ball player who took us to the World Series, my grandfather's reason to live, to hang on.

And hang on he did until October 1960. He and I spent the month in the den huddled over the Emerson transition radio I'd bought with my newspaper money. A makeshift coat hanger antenna was sufficient to pull in the western Pennsylvania radio stations that carried the Pittsburgh teams. Together we listened to hyperbolic announcers blustering over crackling airways when Granddad's Pirates outlasted the New York Yankees in seven games to win the World Series. We leapt into each other's arms when Bill Mazeroski hit his glorious home run to clinch victory in the ninth inning for the Pirates. It was the only time I saw the old man cry. His Pirates, outscored in the series 46 to 21, managed to win four close games against the heavily favored Yankees.

No matter what the rest of my life might bring, I had my moment in the den with my grandfather and my Smoky Burgess catcher's mitt.

Breech Birth

We at Western Shore Press do coffee table books. It's a niche market, not as lame as you might think, stunning photos and light breezy descriptions to occupy uninvited relatives who'd otherwise follow you around the house offering unsolicited advice about your housekeeping. Twenty dollars puts a hefty compendium in your lap, no thinking required, no tacky advertisements. Our first book, *How to Be Self-Sufficient with Three Acres and a Cow*, was scheduled for an October release.

Ours is a family business. I work with my two sisters, Betsy, a silver-tongued TV producer, and Frida, a self-proclaimed Urban Sodbuster. Frida provides the inspiration and Betsy the polish. I contribute a modicum of technical expertise as well as part-time daycare for a pair of three-year-olds, Betsy's girl Denise and Frida's boy Hank.

The business took shape along with the book from a humble beginning at a family barbecue. Clad in my chef's hat and grill master apron, I flipped hamburgers and hotdogs while Betsy and Frida traded war stories of bad male bosses and unappreciated competent women. For the record Betsy no longer had a bad male boss. She'd been laid off from Chesapeake Television in a cost-saving move to transfer profits to management and outsource work to competent women. Frida, unemployed going on several years, was struggling with her three-acre farmette and the *Urban Sodbuster* podcast which she ran from her basement.

"Let's start our own business," Betsy began. "This farmette thing has potential."

"Hopefully something besides too many followers and not enough money."

"You're the idea woman. Let me worry about the business end. That's what I do."

"Where do we start?"

"We need an office and a computer."

Their attention shifted to me where I with the capable assistance of several pre-teens slathered a platter of hotdogs with catsup and mustard.

"Don't look at me. I'm maxed out with my consulting. I'm a people person. I don't actually do any work."

The next afternoon I sat in my office as the odd sibling out in a reply-to-all email exchange where our first big idea took shape. It wasn't an idea but rather four metal clamshell lawn chairs left over from our grandmother's beach house. In Betsy's words: "An authentic urban sodbuster requires vintage outdoor furniture to survey her three-acre farmette." Frida supplied the polka dots and the Rust-Oleum, Betsy the photography and the whimsical description. I give myself credit for photoshopping the end result.

For the next several months, I sat in my attic watching a 24/7 email chain drift across my computer screen as words and images became stories and pages. Several hundred pages of farm scenes and flowery language laid out the tasks required to make three acres self-sustaining. My favorites were a sketch of a pig with garbage-in-bacon-out notation, two mangy sheep churning out enough wool for several Icelandic sweaters, and the restoration of a 1870 bugeye wooden boat we salvaged from the marsh, then donated to the marine museum for a hefty tax deduction.

Halfway through the project both Betsy and Frida announced they were pregnant. Their due dates fit nicely with an October publication date, just in time for the Christmas deluge. Betsy added a photo of two pregnant woman standing in front of the bugeye for the sales brochure.

Several months before publication I was on the phone with the publisher. "Good news," she said. "Chesapeake Television wants to fold your book into a TV series."

"The same Chesapeake Television that laid Betsy off last year?"

"We don't hold grudges in this business."

"I'll check with my sisters and see what they think. Anything else?"

"Our legal department has a problem with the premise. What if somebody believes it's possible to be self-sufficient on three acres?"

"Only an idiot would believe that."

"My mother does. Does that mean she's an idiot?"

"What does legal suggest?"

"A warning message on the fly leaf, something exculpatory."

"Something like 'Warning, this book may cause you to lose your senses and invest your retirement in a few farm animals and a three-acre plot of land.'"

"We'll worry about the wording at this end."

While I was on the phone, the beep-beep-click-click of Frida appeared on the other line. After I hung up, I checked her voicemail. "It's a breech!"

She didn't answer when I called back. I stuffed two toddlers into their OshKosh-B'Gosh sweatsuits and raced over, five miles in four minutes. Why she didn't call for an ambulance,

I didn't know. With no information, I pulled up the driveway. She and her pregnant belly stood over a bleating ewe and its pregnant belly.

"Jesus, what took you so long?"

"Four minutes isn't bad time."

"Roll up your sleeves. Get over here."

I'd been in Frida's barnyard many times, always through the eyes of a visitor, never a participant. As I stepped off the gravel path onto the damp straw she'd thrown over the muck, the smell of musky dust entered my nostrils, penetrating deep into my lungs. No longer an idle listener, I suddenly found myself inside the *Urban Sodbuster* podcast. Frida lifted the ewe's rear leg to expose a tiny hoof protruding a few inches between her legs. "What do you call that?"

"A hoof."

"Also known as a breech."

"What do we do?"

"I don't do anything. I'm pregnant. You reach inside and turn it around."

At this point, the three-year-olds, Hank and Denise, sensed fear on adult faces, fear instead of the usual rock solid, brick shit-house composure they were used to. Both burst into tears. We tried humor to steady our nerves. "How hard can this be?... We're not in Kansas anymore...Don't go looking for a YouTube how-to video."

Humor didn't work. I plopped down beside the ewe and set my phone and watch aside. Frida slowly and deliberately provided instructions. "Reach inside...You're looking for a mouth...Let me know when you find it...This is her fifth lamb... There's plenty of room...Just stretch it a bit."

I slowly accustomed myself to the afterbirth, amniotic fluid, dingle berries, and specks of blood.

My balky start frustrated Frida. "We don't have all day," she grumbled.

I chose not to argue.

"What do you feel?" she asked.

"Ears, definitely ears, and, yeah, a mouth, but no teeth."

"What else?"

"A neck with a snaky thing wrapped around it."

"That's the umbilical cord, not good. See if you can't unwind it."

"Unwind which way?"

"Opposite the way it's wound."

With the head between my thumb and forefinger, I flicked the cord up and over with my pinkie. It wasn't obvious where the lamb stopped and the uterus started.

"It's loose. I looped it over the head."

"Now lift the lamb back up to pull the leg inside, then invert the body without winding the cord."

I found the vocabulary strange, ewe, breech, amniotic, umbilical, but my male brain provided the manual dexterity for which I had no words, lift, turn, snaky, stench.

"It's turned. Now what?"

"Back out slowly. Don't jerk. Don't upset the mother or the lamb."

I let go of the tiny body and slipped my hand out, thankful to be extricated from a less-than-comfortable situation. Before me a tiny head emerged.

"Now what?"

"Back off. Let the mother do the work."

Frida was right. I sat on the ground in sweat, grit, straw, amniotic fluid, and afterbirth as the lamb wormed its way out. This was something I was never taught. As I contemplated the out-of-body experience, Frida barked another order.

"Don't be too smug. You're not finished yet."

She approached me with a Mason jar of disinfectant from which she extracted a pair of scissors. "Trim the umbilical cord two inches away from the lamb's body."

She handed me the scissors and watched carefully as I returned to my midwife role. After I snipped the cord, the ewe took over, licking her lamb clean, but not before she blasted an intense are-you-still-here glare in my direction. I stood up and retreated to a bench alongside the barnyard fence.

The two toddlers joined me, each laying a head against an arm on either side. Neither seemed to mind the blood and guts. For them, this was the new normal. This was how we made sheep. Uncle Henry grovels on the barn floor while Momma Frida barks out orders. Several hours earlier they'd lain down for their afternoon nap in their twenty-first century cocoon. Now they were jerked awake in an eighteenth-century barnyard. Neither made the connection with their respective mothers' delivery in the coming months. Humans are humans. Animals are animals.

Only then did I notice Betsy beyond the fence, camera in her hand, recording for posterity. Submerged in the moment, I hadn't noticed her arrival. Contorting her body from angle to angle as the shutter flickered, she snapped photo after photo: me, the ewe, the lamb, the two toddlers, Frida barking orders. After she joined me on the bench, she set the camera down. "That was amazing. I didn't know you had it in you."

"I didn't even know it existed."

"Not bad for a white male."

"I'll take that as a complement."

Betsy is known for her running commentary on practically everything. It's not as irritating as you might think, an older sister who provides a soothing voice-over narrative in your life. Her stream-of-consciousness was always there. She was always there.

"Looks like we have a cover photo for our book. Trust me. This sells books."

The breech birth story motivated a phone call from our publisher. "That might be over the top. Who'd believe a white male management consultant groveling on the barnyard floor, midwifing a distressed ewe? We're moving the pig with garbage-in-bacon-out notation back to the cover and burying the lamb-ewe piece inside. Whimsy is whimsy. Trust me. I know what I'm doing."

Betsy and her monotone voice-over camped out in my office for the rest of the summer, slowly, steadily steering our book through iteration after iteration: corrections, proofing, fluffing up language, photoshopping for highlights and shadows. "This won't do...too boring...not believable...where did this photo come from? do we have rights to it? the font is too small...the font is too cutesy...the font is too boring."

The fall was a season for births, Betsy in August with an eight-pound boy, Frida in September with a seven-pound girl, and *How To Be Self-Sufficient with Three Acres and a Cow* in October, a ten-pound coffee table book. None was a breech. The next year, Betsy was back at Chesapeake Television producing a new series, *Urban Sodbuster*, featuring her sister

Frida, the consummate three-acre farm woman. I was back in my attic office hawking sensitivity training to clueless managers.

Next Memorial Day, donning my chef's hat and grill master apron, flipping hamburgers for the extended family, I listened as Betsy and Frida plotted our next project. "We should do another book…Can't we just rest on our laurels?…No, we can't… How can we top this?…Wait! I've got it: *How To Be Self-Sufficient Refinishing Antique Lawn Furniture*…That's brilliant."

Over the next year, my three-car garage gradually filled with metal gliders, wrought iron patio chairs, tree-stump stools, wine barrel side tables, hammock rope rockers, and cedar nesting chairs. My computer hard drive was inundated with words and images gradually coalescing into yet another coffee table book.

One pleasant fall evening when we gathered at the farmette to enjoy a glass of wine and watch the sunset, Frida presented me with a sweater that she'd knit from my sheep's wool. Twenty minutes later in the barnyard when I offered him a friendly scratch behind the ear, he snorted at me. My little lamb had become a bully ram with dingle berries dangling from his hairy butt.

Sometimes I wonder who I really am, overpaid consultant to maladjusted executives, midwife to breech birth lambs, babysitter to nieces and nephews, Uncle Henry the grill master, or middle child between two strong-willed sisters. I've grown to accept each role as a part of me. At the end of cool autumn days, when I sit on my patio at sunset in my waffle-knit sweater, when I still sense the amniotic fluid and afterbirth under my fingernails, I shape-shift into an *Urban Sodbuster* midwife. I keep this to myself, because, in the words of my publisher, "Nobody will believe that."

The Oxymoron and the Baltimorean

At 8:30 a.m., on Friday, November 7, 1969, Samuel Edwards sat on the front stoop outside the enlisted barracks at the Signal Corps Training School at Fort Gordon, Georgia. He scratched his bony back through his olive drab fatigue shirt against an army green banister post. One foot was firmly planted on the first step and the other extended, jerking nervously on the brown, sandy walk.

His legs were sore from eight hours of guard duty. The foul odor of hot, itchy feet in scratchy wool socks oozed through the pores of his scuffed, black combat boots. Through the night he'd trudged slowly around the gravel lanes surrounding the wooden structures of the army base. He'd circled the quadrant forty or fifty times, counting the steps, the hours and minutes. When he was relieved of his post, as he headed into the mess hall for bitter black coffee, he noticed his schoolmates gathering on the steps of the EM barracks where the first sergeant barked out names and distributed sheets of paper. "Maffett! Calderon! Thompson! Edwards!"

The clueless draftees milled around the entrance, contemplating individualized sheets of onionskin paper on which fine, crisp letters dictated the events of the coming months. After several months together, they were still more fellows than comrades. Each pimply recruit stared at his orders directing him to report to the Artillery School at Fort Sill, Oklahoma, for two months, and then to board a Boeing 707 for the war overseas. The war overseas was a euphemism for the conflict in the Republic of Vietnam. Sammy's entire class moved along the conveyor belt toward an outpost in the la Drang Valley. Each continued to maintain more mental ties to his hometown, his girlfriend, and his sports teams than to the regimentation and violence that lay ahead. Each dreamed of a return to high school where he might reassume his position in the pecking order.

Before he was inducted into the army, Sammy shared a Read Street row house in Baltimore with Jackie Cessna. She wore blue-collar work shirts over tight sequined jeans and played scratchy Mose Allison LPs on her stereo. He sported a fourteen-hair goatee and dressed in hand-crafted leather sandals and a tie-dye Nehru jacket. For reasons of expediency, they never formalized their relationship into any convention other than a loose bond of sexual companionship and Bohemian brinkmanship. They were too busy being an avant-garde couple to be concerned about bonding and loving. They moved where and when they pleased, distributing aspirin tins of power weed to the pilgrims strolling through the subculture.

None of the individuals gathered on the stoop of the barracks was prepared for the moment. There was always another two-month sojourn at another dusty southern army post. Now their descent of the grand staircase was approaching the final step, Fort Sill, Oklahoma. From there they'd take the final plunge into the pond, get their butts wet wading through the Big Muddy. They were all on the conveyor belt, moving forward and downward.

When Sammy and Jackie were together, they were well suited for the time and place. She emitted bubbly social sparks: Let's go crabbing, let's go bar hopping, let's sparkle, let's go to the beach. All was well until he neglected to register for the fall semester at Towson State University. Within weeks his draft board notified him that his student deferment was terminated.

She and he weren't well suited for separation. During his eight weeks at Fort Bragg and eight weeks at Fort Gordon, he'd been to Baltimore twice. Each trip produced less sparkle, less "let's keep moving" and more "let's have a drink." Everything was slipping away. His golden locks were buzzed onto the linoleum floor at a Fort Bragg barber shop. He needed to rekindle the bond between them, but he had no appreciation for the complexities involved. He sat on the front stoop of the EM barracks, pistol whipped, smacked across the frontal lobes with a sheet of onionskin paper.

Just when his head was ready to explode, he planted his palms on the side rail of the la Drang conveyor belt, vaulted over the edge, and rushed into the barracks to retrieve his Nehru tie-dye jacket from his footlocker. Thirty minutes later he and his hot, itchy feet, his scratchy wool socks, and his scuffed combat boots were on the highway hitchhiking up the East Coast to Baltimore.

The next day Jackie sat at her kitchen table transferring power weed from its Prince-Albert-in-a-Can repository into aspirin tins in anticipation of Fells Point bar hopping that evening. Periodically she practiced a one-handed roll-your-own joint followed by a Marlboro Man kitchen match strike on her blue jeans zipper. Pete Seeger blared on the stereo: "Where have all the soldiers gone, long time passing?" She'd soon receive a special delivery answer to the question.

Shortly before noon Sammy stepped up to her front door unannounced and entered without knocking. No sleep for thirty hours, stubble for hair, sporting a rumpled, tie-dye Nehru over fatigue pants, he was an olive-drab mess. He suffered from sleep deprivation, reality deprivation, Fells Point deprivation, option deprivation, alcohol deprivation, and hair deprivation.

Overly mascaraed eyes met gaunt inductee eyes. They stared at each other in chilly silence, neither prepared for the encounter, not he who had thirty hours to prepare himself, not she who had thirty seconds. Unaware of the NoDoz that sustained him on his long journey, she was under the mistaken impression that a coherent conversation might be possible.

"Do I get a hug?" he asked.

"Not without a shower."

"Aren't you glad to see me?"

"Not unannounced."

"This isn't going well, is it?

"I can't merely flick a mental switch to be back in another man-place."

"At least let me sleep on the couch. We can talk in the morning."

"The answer is no. You can't sleep on the couch."

"It's my couch. I bought it at the thrift store."

Faced with two options, a pointless rambling conversation or him crashing on the couch, she chose the latter. The wretch standing before her bore no resemblance to her quirky boyfriend. She guided him to the living room as he yammered on, "I'm not going back…I'll always love you…we can run away…I'm so sorry…I'm not going back."

"Let's see if we can make you comfortable," she whispered, fluffing dingy thrift store pillows under his head.

He was out cold within minutes. She, on the other hand, experienced a rough night. Their two-year plan to struggle through his extended absence was shattered, replaced by a messy day-to-day outlaw existence. When she slept, her dreams were haunted by guard dogs chasing them through inner-city alleys. When awake, she oscillated between pity and anger, fear and fortitude. All night her slumber was disturbed by background rumblings, the shower, the washer-dryer, the refrigerator, the coffee grinder. She'd slept alone during his four-month absence. Now the masculine scents of cologne, shampoo, and shaving cream permeated her bedroom.

Ignoring her better judgment, she ventured into the living room and shook him awake. "Come to bed, but remember, you're going back tomorrow."

"Okay."

"Okay you'll come to bed, or okay you're going back?"

"Just okay."

She chose not to argue. What difference would one night make? In the morning, he was back in his old man-place, curled up beside her in bed, bagels and lox for breakfast, reading the *Baltimore Sun* at the kitchen table, strumming his guitar on the front stoop. Allowing him back was so easy.

There was another back, Fort Gordon, Georgia, 500 miles to the south where a sheet of onion skin paper lay on his bunk in the EM barracks.

He enjoyed a day of freedom, breakfast in pajamas, afternoon sex, dinner in Little Italy, drinks at Fells Point, smoking weed in front of the *Tonight Show*, morning sex. Midafternoon the next day, reality reentered their lives when the phone rang. She answered. He picked up the extension to listen in. "First Sergeant Donovan here. Am I speaking to Jackie Cessna?"

"You are."

"Do you know why I'm calling?"

"I do."

"Is Sammy there?"

Silence.

"If you see him, tell him if he comes back now, I can fix it. I can pencil him in for an extra travel day. He's due at Fort Sill tomorrow morning at 8:00 a.m., that's eighteen hours. After that, he's on his own, a deserter, think Fort Leavenworth."

Jackie and Sammy sat on the front stoop of her Read Street row house. He scratched his bony back through his tie-dye Nehru coat against a fake brownstone wall. One foot was firmly planted on the first step and the other extended, jerking nervously on the cobblestone walk. She spread a US map across the walk. "Which will it be, big fellow? Fort Sill or Fort Leavenworth?" Big fellow was a euphemism for the 154-pound male, a young male who was eighteen hours from a court-martial for desertion.

She continued, "If we borrow my brother's Thunderbird, we can make it."

"Do I have a choice?"

"Not with me, you don't."

Seventeen hours later they pulled up to the EM barracks of the Artillery School at Fort Sill where his next first sergeant slammed his clipboard on the hood of his jeep and barked out the names of the next class of recruits, "Maffett! Calderon! Thompson! Edwards!"

Sammy grabbed his duffle bag, slipped on his freshly laundered wool socks and spit-shined combat boots, and fell into formation with his classmates. The la Drang Valley conveyer belt lurched forward.

Around the corner Jackie shifted her brother's Thunderbird into overdrive and sped home alone. Two days later she sat at her kitchen table transferring power weed from its Prince-Albert-in-a-Can repository into aspirin tins in anticipation of Fells Point bar hopping.

A Pal's Last Need

Sandy and I were pals, occasional lunches, tennis now and then, confidants in late night phone calls, designated driver when the other drank too much. She typed my term papers. I fixed her car. I called in chits when she needed a plumber. She covered for me when I failed to show for traffic court. We often spoke for hours, my pinball machine of a family, her pinball machine of a love life, both sides embellished with bong, tilt, and gong sound effects.

In the 1970s psychological boundaries had yet to come into vogue. We drew lines in the sand. Sandy's line was, "Don't ruin a perfectly good relationship with romantic entanglements."

Prominent on Sandy's side of the line was her sometimes-on, sometimes-off, sometimes-ex high-school sweetheart Fred, back home in Cleveland. My overprotective sister Jane presided on my side. "Why don't you let me find you an attractive, available girlfriend? This girl is trouble."

Saturday was bread-baking day. Sandy and I met in her kitchen where we churned out the loaf of the week. Her methodology was closer to the dough than mine. She preferred her doorstop KitchenAid mixer, the model replete with dough hook, bread bowl, and grain mill. I worked with a more modest Hamilton Beach bread machine, a bequest from my Aunt Claire's estate. Sandy's secret ingredient was her prize-winning sourdough starter, in her words, "Not just any yeast, but a leaven captured in the church belfry by Belgian monks in the sixteenth century. Mine is the sole surviving strain." My secret was Aunt Claire's cheat sheet, a stash of recipes I found inside her bread machine.

On June 24, 1972, the imaginary line between Sandy and me shifted. I stood at the sink wiping remnants of goo from her dough hook. She leaned over the counter shaping the loaf as only she could. My loaves were lumpy because Aunt Claire's instructions for loaf-shaping were illegibly smeared with oil and crusted dough.

While the bread baked, we sat in silence at the kitchen table, dipping week-old bread into hazelnut coffee. Sandy spoke first. "I need a favor. Are you up to it?"

"Depends on the favor."

"My thesis advisor, promoted to department head, can you believe it?"

"The guy who's been hitting on you?"

"I need a safety date for the celebration tonight."

"You need somebody to run interference?"

"Correct."

"What's the dress?"

11:00 a.m. found us at the Queenstown Outlets where she pieced together my wardrobe for the evening: Clarks penny loafers, Eddie Bauer black turtleneck, Brooks Brothers slacks, all confident but unassuming. She greeted me at the dressing room door. "Damn, you look good. I could kiss you."

Sadly, she didn't kiss me at Brooks Brothers, also not when I emerged from the hair salon shorn of my sideburns and two-day stubble.

Sandy knew how to make an entrance. At 8:45 p.m. she and her newly shorn safety date arrived at the faculty lounge a discreet forty-five minutes late. To complement my paid-escort look, she came dressed as Annie Hall: pleated pants, suspenders, wide tie, tweed vest.

Her thesis advisor assailed her at the door.: "Sandy, where've you been? You know we can't start without you."

"Thank you for having us," she replied in her most droll voice. "You're very kind."

"Heart of my heart, were it more, more would be laid at your feet,"[†] he countered in his most condescending department head voice.

I wasn't impressed. Sandy kicked me in the shin, my cue to step between them. "Preston Humphrey, glad to meet you."

She scooted through the breach I'd opened into the room, cajoling her way across the floor, double kissing everybody French style, left cheek, right cheek, everybody except me and her thesis advisor. He and I stood at the door where he gave me his what's-Sandy-doing-with-a-doofus-like-you look and I responded with a what's-Sandy-doing-with-a-lecher-like-you look. (My sister Jane hates oversexed, controlling men, just an aside.)

This was the classics department at St. Paul, young women discussing Catullus' erotic poetry, penniless scholarship students hovering over the hors d'oeuvres, lanky faculty husbands and bored faculty wives fretting when the interminable party might end, gay men wondering whether Sandy's immaculately groomed safety date was one of them, and archeology majors fuming over the butchered excavation of Troy VI by 19th century Germans. Sandy was the golden girl, National Merit Scholarship, short pixie hair, lean frame, inviting smile, standoff eyes, biting wit, composed beyond belief. In short, unattainable.

Once she was comfortably situated among the German-bashing archaeologists, I set my safety-date duties aside and followed my hormones over to the young women discussing erotic poetry. I was perfunctorily ejected since I'd never read Catullus in the original Latin. With nowhere else to go, I hung out at the bar with civil engineering students abandoned by their Catullus-loving girlfriends. Their conversation revolved around sewerage treatment, how to get rid of sludge in the vernacular.

My least boring conversation came three or four pinot noirs and two plates of Swedish meatballs later when the gay delegation dispatched an envoy to determine whether I was one of them.

"I think Sandy likes you."

I played along. "I'm her buddy."

"… and her escort?"

"We complement each other."

"Do you have a real girlfriend?"

After we consumed thirty minutes parrying unanswered questions and evasive responses back and forth, Sandy appeared to rescue me. "The boy isn't gay. I like him the way he is."

As the night progressed and the crowd thinned, the half-dozen still standing walked across the street to a 24-hour diner for hangover intervention. Shortly after 3:00 a.m, only Sandy and I remained.

"What now?" I asked.

Sandy's eyes toggled between attainable and unattainable. "I need a friend."

I ignored my sister Jane who channeled from the depths, "You always settle for friend."

My question hung in the air. "What now?"

At 5:00 a.m. we settled onto a blanket at the end of the

airport runway, sharing a joint, just enough for a cozy buzz, watching 727s bank in along the bay. We lay still, her face tucked under my shoulder, our fingers intertwined, morning dew settling on our faces.

"Someday..." she whispered but didn't finish her thought.

A few minutes later she continued. "I don't know. Can I make it with you? With us?"

I was along for the ride.

When dawn broke over the broad water, she nestled closer, not her usual elbow in the ribs, but a soft hand on my forearm. "Time to move on."

"What now?"

"Last Wednesday, dusk at tennis, we ran out of quarters for the lights. Let's finish the game."

7:00 a.m. found us at the Elm Street courts, swatting balls back and forth. As usual, I was outclassed. Her forehand was intense and hard, her overhead smash deadly. Her eyes ablaze, her muscles tight, she charged the net on every serve. The best I could do was lob the ball back, setting her up for another slam.

My sister Jane, never one to shy away from sports analogies, once observed: "She's a pounder. You're a lobber. Why do you do this to yourself?"

Two sets and nine games later Sandy had me cornered, match point, her advantage, she serving. We were both exhausted, both determined to see it through. She needed one final ace to put me away. Somehow, I managed a return, a soft, easy lob into her forehand. With me out of position, all she needed was a gentle tap into the forecourt. POW. The ball sailed over the fence into the brambles. We never finished the game. She collapsed on the court. I knelt beside her where we sat in silence. My mind toggled: Should I approach? Should I not? My question was answered when she shifted her hand from my forearm to my thigh.

At 9:00 a.m. we stood on her front porch.

"What now?" I asked.

Her inner classics major rose to the fore. "Vivamus, mea Lesbia, atque amemus."[†]

"You've lost me."

"Latin for 'Time to settle up at the favor bank.'"

Her enchanting deposit consumed both of us for several hours. The Catullus-swooning women from the classics department could only dream of the experience behind the poems. For a few brief hours, our line in the sand dissipated into drunken kisses, shoulder rubs, entwined limbs, acrobatic sex, and bellowing moans. We lay in each other's arms, snoozing, floating, kissing, stroking.

Shortly after noon she kissed me on the cheek. "You awake?"

"Barely."

She squeezed my hand, scooted closer. Her words came softly, deliberately, "I'll be away for a while, back to Cleveland to end things with Fred, tie up loose ends."

I liked the end-things-with-Fred part, but not the away-for-a-while part. "When do you leave?"

"Soon."

"Today?"

"I have to go."

"Get some sleep first. It's been a long night."

With that she settled back into my arms. We lay still, at times affectionate, at times exhausted, mostly asleep. When I awoke, she was gone. I squinted to make out the digits on the bedside clock, a blurry 7:00 a.m. After taking a few minutes to scoop up my clothes strewn across the bedroom floor, after a quick trip to the bathroom to empty my bladder, I found her in the kitchen, sipping coffee, writing a note. She wore her familiar jeans and tie-dye T-shirt. Her overstuffed duffel bag lay beside the door. I poured myself a cup and sat down opposite her. She slid the note across the table and watched as I read.

> *Once a week on Sunday morning, retrieve the sourdough starter from your refrigerator and discard all but one-half cup. Then add one cup of King Arthur bread flour and one cup of lukewarm water. Mix with a wooden spoon, cover, then return to the refrigerator where the cold temperature will slow the fermentation. The starter will continue to rise, but extremely slowly. I've included a spreadsheet where you can record your progress and a refrigerator thermometer. Your refrigerator should be set to 37 degrees.*

"What do you think?" she asked.

I pushed the note back to her. "Your cursive is flawless."

She spoke slowly. "You're the one person I can trust."

"With your starter?"

"... and my heart."

"Do you have to go?"

"I've a history in Cleveland."

"With Fred?"

"Trust me. I'll be back."

"Can you stay another day? For us? For me?"

"I have to go."

"You're exhausted. We're both exhausted."

"I'll pull over if I have to."

"It's 400 miles. Eight hours."

Throughout the conversation my inner sister Jane waited patiently, ready to swoop in. "Once a month! How long does it take to dump a boyfriend?" she shouted in my ear. I shoved her back into her alcove.

Tears in her tired eyes, Sandy escorted me to the front door where she entrusted me with her precious yeast. With one hand dragging her duffle bag and the other clutching my arm, she walked me down the driveway to our cars. There, after planting a few staccato pecks on my cheek, she slid the duffle bag into her back seat, then a few more hugs and she pushed us apart. "We'll be okay, you and me, together soon."

"Last night was a good start."

She tightened her grip on my arm. Her voice dropped an octave into a rote contralto. "Feed my starter. I'll make it worth your while."

Jane cleared her throat deep from within her alcove. "It won't be easy for her to part with the notoriously self-serving Fred. These high school sweethearts don't go quietly."

I watched from the curb as Sandy headed out West Street in her VW Beetle, embarking on a long, hard journey.

She never made it to Cleveland. Her drive ended on the exit lane off the Pennsylvania Turnpike onto Interstate 80.

When I returned home from my evening job at the bookstore, two messages flashed on my answering machine.

4:45 p.m. Sandy from a pay phone outside Pittsburgh: "Last night was a dream. I miss you already. You're the best."

9:21 p.m. Jane: "Sorry to do this on the answering machine.

I want you to hear it from me. Sandy's mother called. You weren't listed in the phone book. I was the only Humphrey she could find. There was a crash. Sandy didn't make it. Her VW drifted into the path of a truck loaded with treated lumber. Call me back. I need to hear your voice."

The accident report from the Pennsylvania Highway Patrol speculated that she fell asleep at the wheel. Perhaps her mind wandered to our long, exhausting night together. Perhaps she was preoccupied, rehearsing her break-up conversation with Fred. Most probably she fell asleep.

The next morning after a sleepless night I found myself alone in my apartment contemplating the unthinkable, my first day without Sandy. Too numb to cry, too stunned to think, only one place to go, I sat down at the kitchen table to feed her starter. When I finished, it seemed only logical to bake a loaf of bread. Aunt Claire's bread machine clunked along on its worn bearings, kneading, kneading, kneading.

As I stood to pour myself a second cup of coffee, the doorbell rang.

"Who is it?" I yelled.

"Jane."

"The door's open."

She picked up my half-eaten bagel. "You gonna eat this?"

"Help yourself."

"What are you doing?" she asked, sitting down. "More to the point, how are you doing?"

"Baking bread."

"I can make BLTs for lunch if you're interested."

After a trip to the Amish market for tomatoes and lettuce, Jane spent the morning cleaning my apartment. For some reason, I didn't mind. She was welcome company considering the day, my first without Sandy. Over time a new ritual fell into place. The first Tuesday of every month Jane arrived midmorning with tomatoes, lettuce, and bacon. She cleaned my apartment while I baked. We settled at the lowest common denominator: BLTs with fresh sourdough bread.

Over lunch several months out, I shared Sandy's last words. "Feed my starter. I'll make it worth your while." Jane was surprisingly empathetic, not a word about finding me an attractive, available girlfriend; no "I told you this girl was trouble."

She simply leaned forward across the kitchen table and squeezed my hand. Having grown up in the same household as me, the household where our father read poetry aloud at the breakfast table, she shared one of his favorite quotes:

"A pal's last need is a thing to heed."[†]

◄ ◄ ◄ ◄

Footnotes for "A Pal's Last Need"

Page 29:
"Heart of my heart, were it more, more would be laid at your feet,"
Algernon Charles Swinburne: "The Oblation," 1871.

Page 32:
"Vivamus, mea Lesbia, atque amemus."
Catullus (c84–54 B.C.): "Let us live, my Lesbia, and let us love."

page 36:
"A pal's last need is a thing to heed."
Robert Service: "The Cremation of Sam McGee," *The Spell of Yukon,* 1907.

Get Out of Jail Free

Triple witching, four days a year, the third Fridays of March, June, September, and December when stock options, stock index futures, and stock index options all expire, days when wealth flows from victimized retail traders to savvy institutional profiteers, from the unprepared to the prepared. I'm both fortunate to consider myself among the ranks of the prepared and ashamed to be a profiteer.

On Friday morning, June 21, 2019, I sat at my desk at Southern Maryland Wealth Management, psyching myself for the onslaught. I was prepared: Spreadsheets and computer terminals locked and loaded. All phone calls blocked, no outside stimulation. Only the privileged few who know my cell phone number dared penetrate my cocoon. They'd been warned: "Somebody better be dead or in the emergency room before I'm interrupted."

I'm completely engaged in my morning ritual when the phone rings. Against my better judgment, I answer. "This better be good!"

"Daddy, my car was stolen."

"Are you sure it wasn't towed? This has happened before."

"That wasn't my fault. There should be a thirty-minute grace period."

"Did you leave the keys in the ignition?"

"Maybe."

What my daughter means is, the Honda Accord I loaned her years ago was stolen. My first thought is to hope this extremely boring masterpiece of Japanese engineering has found its way to chop-shop heaven where only the insurance company has to worry about it. We talk for a few more minutes, me grumbling, her crying, our usual dysfunctional exchange.

Several days later, I stand in my kitchen, next to my coffee press, hand on the plunger, eyes on the wall clock.

The phone rings.

"Yes."

"Mr. Kershaw?"

"Speaking."

"The county police found your car."

"Is there a problem?"

"Car's fine. They picked it up staking out the bad guys."

"Bad guys have my car?"

"Not anymore. The car's at the impoundment lot. We need your help."

"With the car?"

"No, with the bad guys. You'll be hearing from us."

Once I recover from the interruption, I pour myself a cup of coffee and retire to the patio to regain my composure. My composure must wait. The doorbell rings. A police officer hands me an envelope.

"Mr. Peter Kershaw, registered owner of a silver 2009 Honda Accord. You are requested to appear in person at the courthouse in Rockville on the morning of June 24, 2017, at 9:00 a.m. If you fail to appear, a deputy will be dispatched to secure your presence."

Heretofore my insecure presence has appeared in court only for an embarrassing number of divorce hearings.

Tuesday morning, I arrive at the courthouse, where a large officer at the security desk confiscates my Dietz & Watson corned-beef sandwich, my kosher dill pickle, and my fingernail clippers. He tut-tuts as he slams my backpack onto his conveyer belt, failing to notice a flask of single malt whiskey, cleverly nestled inside.

At the next checkpoint I encounter a platinum blond policewoman with a large revolver strapped to her hip-hugging uniform trousers.

"State your business."

"I'm here because my car was stolen."

I hand her my summons. She whistles a gallows tune under her breath as she reads, then picks up her walkie-talkie and summons a linebacker-class bailiff who accompanies me to a cloakroom overlooking the court proceedings. He grabs a walkie-talkie from his weaponry-laden belt and summons prosecuting attorney Sarah McNichol.

"Thanks for coming. Our subpoenas don't work very often."

I make a mental note to ignore the next subpoena.

She turns to leave, then faces me again, this time with fear in her eyes. "Watch out for this guy. He's threatened all of us, said he'd go after our kids."

"Why me?" I ask.

"His lawyer was betting you'd not show up. The bad guy has a right to confront his accuser."

She directs my attention through the bulletproof glass to the judge below who shuffles case after case along his own well-oiled conveyer belt. One by one the other witnesses are summoned to the podium for their lame testimony and subsequently dismissed into civilian heaven.

My case is last. I watch through the window as two police officers drag a wild man into the courtroom and seat him at the defendant's table, where he yells obscenities at the judge.

After he calms down, his lawyer, the prosecutors, and the judge convene at the bench. I hunker down in my seat when they turn their attention to me in the witness room.

An hour later, one of several tightly wrapped police officers, I've lost track of which one, returns with his cohorts who shake my hand. A wiry, buzz-cut sergeant grabs my hand in his gamekeeper knuckles and squeezes his appreciation. "We can't thank you enough. The bad guy has asked for a jury trial."

I give him my now-what look.

"Don't worry. That'll never happen. If you hadn't showed up for court today to testify, he'd have walked away free. Based on your appearance, we can lock him up for a few weeks until we charge him for aggravated assault with a deadly weapon. You bought us the time we need to make an airtight case. He has threatened police officers and their families. You stepped up, and for that, we thank you."

"Can I go now?"

"Not yet. The captain wants to see you."

I'm led across the street to another courtly building where Captain Donovan extends his gargantuan hand and motions for me to sit.

"Mr. Kershaw, I can't thank you enough. If there is ever anything I can do for you, let me know."

"Anything like?"

"Speeding tickets, parking tickets, ballpark tickets, you name it. I hear there's a Bette Midler concert at Wolf Trap this weekend. I can get you front row seats."

He pulls out his business cards and scribbles on the back for a few minutes before handing me the note, the gist of which reads: "Get Out of Jail Free."

After the tow truck follows me home with my Honda trailing behind, I inspect the trunk, where the bad guy has assembled a mishmash of stereo equipment, recreational drugs, and Ray Charles records. My daughter's boyfriend is an electronics wizard. He splices the contents of the trunk into an amazing sound system.

The next year my ex-wife's son is pulled over on the beltway in his mother's canary-yellow Corvette, clocked at 97 mph approaching the American Legion Bridge from the Maryland side. At 30 mph over the speed limit, he faces jail time. His mother calls me in tears, "Don't let my baby go to jail. Fix this, and I'll give you anything you want, and I mean anything."

Later that afternoon, I scrounge through my cache of other people's business cards and extract my "Get Out of Jail Free Card." A quick phone call to Captain Donovan, and my stepson's paperwork disappears.

I don't follow up on his mother's intriguing offer. Occasionally, though, I feel lonely when I stand in my boxer briefs beside the kitchen counter, hand on the plunger, Trader Joe's Columbian in the hopper, sunrise on the patio. I take a peek at Captain Donovan's business card to which I've paper-clipped two Wolf Trap passes and a promissory note: "Anything you want, and I mean anything."

Mom Takes a Fall

The bedroom door creaked open. A gray head peeped in. I lay in the bottom berth of a bunk bed under a deep, feathery comforter stitched with butterflies and bluebirds. This wasn't my bed or my room. I squinted in the twilight to make out the face at the door. My Aunt Beth stepped into the room.

"Any takers for breakfast?"

This wasn't the Aunt Beth I knew, the spouter of platitudes on the sort of breakfast growing boys need. This Aunt Beth exuded fear and uncertainty.

Another face appeared, peering down from the upper bunk. My sister Susan answered as if I weren't there. "Peanut butter toast. That's all he'll eat."

She shinnied down the ladder where she took charge in her most polished imitation of an adult.

"Wake up, Burt. We'll miss the school bus!"

I spotted my clothes neatly folded on the side bench. Mom never folded my clothes. I disappeared under the comforter. "I can't get dressed in front of you."

Aunt Beth backed out of the bedroom, allowing me a few minutes of privacy.

"We'll see you at breakfast."

Susan scooped up her clothes from the side bench and headed for the bathroom. Ten minutes later I poked my head around the corner from the hallway into the kitchen. My place setting at the table needed no name card: peanut butter on raisin bread toast, a small glass of orange juice, and a neatly folded napkin. Aunt Beth allowed only mitered corners on her linen.

Uncle Robbie manned the griddle, churning out scrambled eggs and sausage links; the maestro himself conducting with his spatula, nothing up his sleeve, nothing in his chef's hat, until, presto, a farm fresh egg appeared behind my ear, a double yolk, then another, and another. Soon six eggs were in the air at one time. Tempted beyond my six years, I changed my order to french toast dipped into nutmeg and cinnamon.

Aunt Beth took her seat at her end of the table, two poached eggs timed to perfection on sliced halves of English muffin. We bowed our heads while she prayed. "May you watch over our sister Sandy and deliver her back to us."

The last thing I remember was my otherwise healthy mother tucking me in under my cowboy and Indian comforter. The next morning, she needed our prayers, no explanation for what, how, why, or when. While we ate, the school bus tooted its horn at the bottom of the lane. Uncle Robbie opened the front door to wave the driver on. "I'll take you kids to school. It's on my way."

Seconds later, my cousin Jamie dashed down the hall and grabbed his book bag on the way out the door.

"The bus just left," Uncle Robbie said. "Sit down and enjoy your breakfast."

Jamie returned to the kitchen. "Why are they here?"

Aunt Beth spoke slowly. "Their mother's sick. They'll be with us for a while."

"What happened?"

"She fell. We don't know why."

"Where's she now?" I asked.

"With your father at the hospital."

My feet dangled from the adult chair. "I need my other shoes. We play ball at recess."

Aunt Beth glanced at the leather shoes she'd laid out and nodded to Uncle Robbie. He rummaged through my duffle bag for sneakers.

"And my ball mitt."

"We'll stop by your place on the way to school."

My mother and Uncle Robbie built houses on adjoining parcels of their grandfather's apple orchard in the hills above Frostburg in western Maryland. Uncle Robbie drove us down his driveway across the street and up our driveway to our house. I opened the car door and jumped out. "I'll run in."

"We'll come with you," he said, rushing to catch up. Susan followed. Jamie stayed in the car.

Our golden retriever Rusty met us at the door. Spike, the mutt, remained asleep on the couch, a liberty he took in Mom's absence. Uncle Robbie instinctively stroked his floppy ears. "Been sleeping on the couch, eh boy?"

The living room was a mess. The floor lamp lay overturned on the floor. Blood now crusted had dripped over the edge of the coffee table onto the carpet. Susan picked up the lamp and dabbed at the blood with a paper towel. Uncle Robbie pulled her back. "We'll take care of that later."

They tussled with the paper towel roll, both upset, surprised at the other's insistence. Finally, Susan gave in and allowed Uncle Robbie to lead her out the door. I followed, smacking the pocket of my baseball mitt with my fist.

That evening Aunt Beth pressed us for our feelings. "Let it out. She's your mother."

Naturally Susan came prepared with a litany of socially acceptable feelings, all of which I felt, but less articulately. "We'll pull together for Mom's sake, be strong, meet the bus on time every day, feed and brush the dogs."

"That's nice, Honey, but how do you feel inside? Are you scared?"

"We're fine. I'll take care of Burt and Dad."

Then turning to me, Aunt Beth asked, "And you, young man? Do you have anything you want to talk about?"

My first inclination was to curl up on the couch with the dogs. My second choice was escape into recess. But my words came out differently. "I'll take out the trash."

While Aunt Beth grilled me, Susan sat at the dining room table where she directed her excess energy toward my disheveled book satchel. She aligned my homework assignments across the table and began to fill in the blanks on the worksheets as if her flawlessly executed block letters could pass for my scribbling.

I searched my brain for an emotion acceptable to Aunt Beth. "I wish Dad was here. We'd run out to the barn and work on the old apple press."

Aunt Beth patted me on the head. "That's a good start. What else?"

That was all I had, but I slogged forward through the conversation. "I want Mom home with us."

"I know it hurts," she said.

Uncle Robbie saved me from further interrogation when he returned from the hospital with an update. "She fell. We don't know why. She'll stay at the hospital tonight. They'll move her to Hopkins Medical Center tomorrow."

I searched his pale face for an explanation. Bewilderment was all he had to offer. My desire to curl up with the dogs intensified.

"When's Dad coming home?" I asked.

Uncle Robbie put his hand on my shoulder, "I'll talk to him in the morning, before we leave for Baltimore."

Dad stopped by to check on us at bedtime. "I know you kids'll do your share. I know you'll watch out for each other while I'm gone."

"We will," Susan promised. "You know we will."

Dad turned to me, "How about my little man here?"

"Okay," was the only word I could muster.

After bedtime, I crept back down the hall to eavesdrop on the adult conversation in the kitchen. The symptoms spewed forth. "Dizziness...vomiting...headache...disorientation."

That's when it got dicey. I couldn't see Aunt's Beth's arm gestures without divulging my hiding place, but her voice was clear. "It's that damned scrap metal center that did it. You could smell the place for twenty miles. While you boys served in the Pacific during the war, your sister worked at the Savage River junkyard, extracting scrap metal from old cars and trucks, a nasty and dangerous job."

Aunt Beth wasn't finished. Before Uncle Robbie could voice an opinion, she continued her tirade. "Don't give me that business about how easy we had it on the home front. Your sister was stuck in the junkyard sniffing every solvent you can imagine while you boys tooled around the Pacific in your big fancy boats."

"They weren't big fancy ships. They were destroyer escorts, tight quarters on small boats. I was seasick for three years."

"It's your sister who's sick now. Your damned war put her there, a man's war. She deserves as much credit as the rest of you. She didn't sit around in her seersucker dress waiting for the boys to come home. You know that, don't you?"

My hiding place seemed secure until Susan crawled into the alcove beside me with a shush finger on her lips. Her shush was a bit more vocal than she intended. Uncle Robbie glanced in our direction. "What was that?"

He pulled back the curtain, slipping into his jovial uncle voice. "Eavesdroppers! Just as I suspected."

Before I knew it, Aunt Beth stood over us, prodding us for our feelings again. This time I had a ready-made answer. "I miss my dogs."

Susan's thoughts had evolved since our last feelings session, and her face showed it. "I wish somebody'd tell me the truth," she said.

Uncle Robbie chose to answer my question. "The dogs stay put in your house. We'll check on them tomorrow. We don't want to stress them anymore that we have to."

Aunt Beth faced Susan directly. "Your mother fell. We don't know why."

"I want the real truth. The truth about the junk yard and the war."

Aunt Beth faced Susan directly. "We know things now we didn't know then. Our country needed metal to make guns and boats. Your mother worked at the junk yard to recover metal from all sorts of trash. She didn't protect herself from the chemicals they used."

"Is that why they put her in the hospital?"

"We can't say that for sure, but probably, yes."

The next day Uncle Robbie accompanied Dad to Baltimore for Mom's exploratory surgery. "I'll drive," Dad announced, climbing in behind the wheel. Uncle Robbie tugged the car keys from his hand and guided him into the passenger seat. Dad never allowed anyone else to drive his Lincoln. Today was different. He passively slipped into the passenger seat.

They returned late Friday night after our bedtime. Again, I snuck into my hiding spot beneath the stairs. I cringed as Uncle Robbie delivered the diagnosis. "It's definitely a brain tumor, hopefully not malignant. A minor incision through the eye socket was all they'd risk. We won't know if they got it all. A biopsy will tell."

"Sandy can take it. If anyone can pull through this, it's my sister." Uncle Robbie reassured them.

"She'll be fine. She's in the Lord's hands," Aunt Beth said.

"Don't forget the surgeon," Uncle Robbie said. "He has hands too."

For the next several weeks, dreams came and went, Mom grabbing the lamp as she fell, blood dripping from the coffee table onto the rug. tumors advancing and retreating, centimeters, millimeters, all measurements foreign to my frame of reference.

I grew accustomed to a transposed life with my aunt and uncle and my cousin Jamie. I lost touch with the images of my life at home with Mom and Dad before Mom's fall.

Then one day the clouds lifted. Just before bedtime Aunt Beth herded Susan and me into the dining room for yet another heart-to-heart talk. Uncle Robbie and Dad returned from the hospital in Baltimore.

"They got it all. The tumor's gone. She'll be okay." Dad announced with a smile on his face.

Uncle Robbie followed him into the room. "Correction: They may have gotten it all. The tumor wasn't malignant, but there's no guarantee it won't reappear tomorrow or ten years out. She's with us now. That's the important thing. We take it one day at a time."

Aunt Beth incorporated the news into our feelings session. "She's ours to enjoy while we can, hopefully for a long time."

Saturday morning, I awoke to find my dog Spike sleeping at the foot of my bed. I leaned up to discover there weren't any butterflies or bluebirds imprinted on my comforter. I was back with my old dingy cowboy-and-Indian comforter, back in my own room with the matching Wild West curtains.

I found Mom in the living room. She wore her familiar old bathrobe but with a pink scarf over her head. When she turned to greet me, the reason for the scarf emerged: An unhealed scar extended over the side of her left eye. Her strawberry blond hair was shaved on the front of her scalp. Dark glasses covered her blackened eyes. The left lens was thick like an old man's glasses.

I faced her head on. She was back, but her face was scary, her eyes recessed, her head shaved. She leaned forward to hug me, but I ran from the house, retreating to the barn where I tinkered with the apple press, to be anywhere but in the arms of my mother.

Psych Wing

Edward Billotte, sessions once a month, I saved him for the end of the day. He demanded too much, left nothing for my other patients. He began each encounter with the same defiance, faced me from the couch, centered a sandstone coaster on the coffee table, twisted open a bottle of cherry Coke, trickled it down the side of his glass, pulled a flask of light sweet rum from his hip pocket, stiffened his drink, centered his glass on the coaster.

"Cuba Libre," he explained.

Tattoos on his forearm, a scar on the back of his hand, another on his cheek, he slid a yellow pencil from behind his ear, tapped the side of his glass, syncopation, silence where a voice should be.

Every session the same standoff, the same fruitless sparring. I retreated behind my poker face, he behind his two-day stubble. I poured myself a cup of strong black tea, slipped a binder from my satchel, read aloud. "Staff Sergeant Edward Billotte, thirty-three years old, high school graduate, three years at West Virginia University before dropping out to enlist in the military, two tours in Vietnam, Distinguished Service Medal, possible PTSD but no confirmed diagnosis, honorable discharge, Fort Bragg, April 1973, divorced twice, currently unemployed."

He stared at my diplomas on the wall, read aloud, "Dr. Elizabeth Walcott, Bachelor of Science from Notre Dame University, M.D. from Stanford University, Residency in Psychiatry at Baylor University, Consulting Physician at the Martinsburg Veterans Hospital."

He leaned back with a smirk and set the flask on the table. "Help yourself. It takes the edge off."

"Is that necessary?" I asked.

"Why not? You've tried everything else."

I reached for the flask, then hesitated.

"Go ahead," he dared me. "No one else wants your job parsing out dribbles of sanity to whacked vets."

I reached for the flask and spiked my tea with light sweet rum. "What do you have for me today?" I asked.

"You'll have a field day with this one."

I leaned back in my chair, pen and binder ready. "Go on."

He leaned forward, eyes softer than usual, lips looser, a faint smile. "Remember last November when you fired me?"

"I didn't fire you. I suggested we take a break, that you go away for a while. Your obvious goal was to outsmart me, toy with me. You're welcome back when you're ready to work."

"I took your advice on the away-for-a-while part."

"Go on."

He adjusted the sandstone coaster, recentered his Coke, leaned back in the sofa, spoke slowly, "You'll think this is a dream."

"I won't know until I hear it."

"Key West, I'd never been there, seemed like a good place to get away."

"Go on."

> I planned to take the ferry from Fort Myers to Key West, Jimmy Buffet on the jukebox, a Corona in my hand, a duffle bag at my side. I drove straight through from Morgantown to Fort

Myers. This put me at the ferry landing the day before my reservation, time enough for a quick loop through the Everglades. The night clerk at my motel hooked me up with his brother-in-law who ran boat tours.

I arrived an hour before the scheduled departure. As other passengers arrived, my distaste for crowds quickly set in. When a Bermuda-short clad family with four brash kids squeezed onto the bench beside me, I decided on the solo canoe trip into the mangroves, this despite warning from the dispatcher and the dock boy about the confusing labyrinth of passages among the islands.

I should have listened. Later that afternoon I found myself paddling fiercely across an open stretch of water to stay ahead of an unexpected squall. When the opportunity arose, I ducked into a passage through dense mangrove. The storm never abated. I slept in the canoe overnight, munching crackers, sipping Jack Daniels, spraying mosquitoes with Deep Woods DET. I struggled to form my poncho into a makeshift tent through a night of water lapping on the canoe, deep-throated bird calls, and thunder.

The next morning, I awoke cold and wet. I raised my head above the gunwale into a dense fog that obscured all points of reference. I lay back down, head on my wet backpack, and fell back to sleep.

My next memory was a slight woman poking me in the shoulder.

"Thank God that I found you. Come. We're late."

Together we dragged my canoe through the knee-deep water onto a path that led to her car, a small Renault station wagon. After we secured the canoe onto the roof rack, she motioned me into the passenger seat. I was along for the ride, but at least it was a ride. We drove for hours in silence on a gravel road. She looked straight ahead, hands tightly gripping the steering wheel without acknowledging me. When she did speak, she spoke in French, curses, comments on the ruts, musings how deep the puddles on the road might be.

When we arrived in town, I found myself in the rear seat half asleep. The driver turned a corner onto a side road and waved to an older woman on the curb. She opened the door and motioned me out. I stumbled when my backpack caught on the seatbelt.

She grabbed me by the arm and scolded. "I've been looking for you. Where have you been?"

"She dismissed the driver and led me to a park bench, holding my hand. "It took a while, but I found you. I was sent to escort you home, to ease your way back."

Only then did I notice where I was: a Vietnamese village.

"Aren't you a little late for that?" I asked her. Then I added, "I've done okay."

"Are you hungry?" she asked.

"I could use a bite."

"She motioned to a young boy who was pushing his bicycle through the park. He approached when she beckoned with her hand. He leaned over to hear her soft whisper. She handed him a few coins, and he was off on his bicycle. He returned a few minutes later with shrimp cakes and dipping sauce.

We sat on a bench on the bank of a stream, eating and talking.

She took my hand as she spoke, "You've had a rough time, haven't you? You don't have to be alone, to make it on your own. There are others you can trust if you listen. You don't have to be so brave. You're not very good at it. Find others who are like you, who've experienced what you experienced. Don't lock them out. You can't control everything, not even yourself. Accept the pain. It's become part of you."

She knew my thoughts before I did, the inside of my mind. I was frozen, unable to talk, to tell her that I'd managed, that I'd made my own way back.

"You're tired," she said, leaning forward, laying me down on the bench. I remember the dark clouds drifting overhead, the rain soft on my face. She sat with me as I fell asleep. I can still feel her warm hand on my chest. She draped a dry blanket over me, shielding me from the rain. When I awoke, I was back in my canoe. The rain had passed. In the distance I saw the lights of the town. I could make my way back.

When he finished his story, Eddie turned to me. "All this was real, the warmth of her hand, her soft voice, the rain on my face."

I leaned forward and placed my hand over his scar. "Maybe the woman is part of you," I suggested.

For the first time ever, Eddie didn't jerk his hand back. "I knew you'd say that. She's not inside me. She's real."

"Sent from a place where they watch out for people like you? Maybe that place is a part of you."

"She touched me. I felt her hand on mine, warmth."

"She searched for you for years. Then you mysteriously appeared in a Vietnamese village on your tour through the Florida Everglades."

"That's it."

"Did you see trees, telephone poles, ponds, heron? Was it a real place? A transcendental place?"

"Are you asking whether there were old men in white robes, philosophizing with one another?"

"I'm asking if this is one of your games, if you're making this up."

"She said that the elders sent her. I take her at her word."

"Let's concentrate on the woman. Did you meet her only the one time?"

"She's with me. I feel her."

"Did you touch her? How did she feel?"

"Are you asking whether I have an imaginary friend, a friend who may or may not be a part of me, a friend who was sent from an imaginary place, which also may or may not be a part of me?"

"You know what I'm asking."

"She comforted me, reassured me. When she held my hand, I felt energy, peace I haven't felt in years."

"I'm asking whether you're okay today, now, right here in my office."

"You think this is a dream, don't you?"

"Doesn't matter what I think."

"You think I'm toying with you?"

"Doesn't matter. Bringing you back, that's what matters."

"I made my way back."

"But did you find your way home? I can help you with that if you let me."

"That's why I'm here."

"No more toying, no more outsmarting?"

"That's why I'm here."

"We can work with that."

A Touchy Subject

A new kitchen,
a simple concept,
 appliances functioning properly,
 counter space deep and wide,
 bar and stools where friends sit
 to chat up the cook,
 bright light when it's needed,
 gadgets galore tucked away
 in hand-hewn cabinets.

In the words of my sister Susan, "If I hear one more word about that damned kitchen, I'll explode. This project never ends, old cabinets piling up in the dumpster, kitchen floor ripped up, no place to set the toaster, fridge relegated to the entrance hall. I'm suffocating."

In the words of my wife Toni, putzing around in our 1950s' formica kitchen, "Your sister doesn't know how lucky she is, hardwood cabinets instead of laminate, stainless-steel appliances, Mexican tile floors. I can only dream of a kitchen like that. I don't understand her. She planned her new kitchen for years. Now she feels suffocated, whatever that means."

In the words of my sister-in-law Pam, who had lost husband, house, kitchen, sobriety, and career after her daughter died, "Your sister has no concept of suffocation. She doesn't understand the dark abyss where you can't breathe."

In the words of Susan's husband Sammy, "I thought it's what she wanted. One day she's ecstatic over the new kitchen. The next she's never home, working late at the library."

In the words of Professor David Allen PhD, Susan's not-so-clandestine lover and repartee-spewing dissertation advisor, "You people don't understand. Susan needs intellectual stimulation. Mexican tile floors and stainless-steel cabinets don't work. She needs a new kitchen like she needs a hole in the cranium."

As you can see,
    a kitchen upgrade
        is a touchy subject
            in our family.

A Road Trip

My day begins when I depress the plunger on my stainless-steel coffee press and send a stream of 190-degree water through freshly ground Trader Joe's Columbian. Ten minutes later I sit on my patio to enjoy breakfast and read the *Washington Post*. Occasionally I set the newspaper aside to admire my vegetable garden: straight rows of sugar snap peas inching up a stainless-steel trellis, pumpkin vines snaking through the fence across the lawn, tomato cages protecting my own hybrid seedlings, and garden implements meticulously organized in my board-and-batten shed. Here I find the quiet where I can enjoy the scent of lavender and basil in my herb garden, the fluted call of the wood thrush in the oak grove, and the flutter of swallow-tails in my butterfly bush.

Last year, on the occasion of my sixty-fifth birthday, my granddaughter's ninth grade art class surprised me with a fresh coat of paint. My shed is now replete with yellow and pink daisies, ruby-throated hummingbirds sipping nectar from columbine, a distant pond with a bullfrog peeping through cattails, a border of wisteria framing the scene, and, to top it all off, a hex sign to ward off groundhogs, moles, and rabbits.

One morning not long ago, after ceremoniously completing my morning ritual, I entered the garden shed to select a suitable insecticide to combat the latest infestation of squash bugs in my pumpkin patch. Just as I reached for a canister of biodegradable insect spray, my answering service called. I shifted gears into my business voice. "I'm in a meeting. Can this wait?"

"You don't want to wait for this."

I listened as the receptionist pulled up one message after another:

7:19 a.m. Mr. Whitman, the director of your uncle's assisted living: Your Uncle Frank has escaped. The United Parcel driver left his truck running in the circular drive while he ferried packages into the lobby. Frank drove off with the truck. We need your help.

7:35 a.m. Your Aunt Diane: He's wandered off again, something about finding his mother's teaberry still.

8:05 a.m. Mr. Whitman again: I talked to the Lavale station of the Highway Patrol. They've issued a silver alert.

8:22 a.m. Corporal Eisenburger with the Oakland, Maryland, police: We picked your uncle up at McDonald's where he stopped for breakfast. The delivery truck was wedged under the drive-thru arches. United Parcel won't press charges if nothing is missing. McDonald's was equally forgiving. They don't sue confused older citizens, bad for business.

8:30 a.m. Margaret Peterson, case worker at assisted living: You're listed as a secondary contact. After an uninformative discussion with your Aunt Diane and a message-queue-full recording on your cousin Jamie's phone, we're moving you up to primary. We need to talk about your uncle's cognitive problems. He seems to be lost in the 1930s.

8:35 a.m. Uncle Frank: Come pick me up, your grandmother's teaberry still, we need to find it before it's too late.

Three hours and 139 miles later, I pulled into the parking lot of the Oakland Police Department. The municipal building was empty, but a note on the dispatcher's desk directed me to the library across the street. Uncle Frank sat at the library reference desk talking to a woman.

"Your uncle is a remarkable man," she said when I introduced myself. "We've had an interesting discussion."

"You're not with the police department?"

"I'm the librarian, Mrs. Eisenburger. The boys asked me to watch Frank while they went to lunch."

"Any relation to Corporal Eisenburger?"

"He's my son."

"They left Uncle Frank with you?"

"Are you asking if I can handle the job?"

"No, just wondering what your job is, if Uncle Frank's in trouble."

"No, he's right where he should be."

"In Oakland, Maryland?"

"Yes, with the one person who still knows what a teaberry still is."

"That can wait. I'm here to escort—"

"—your uncle back to assisted living. I don't think so. He doesn't want to go back."

Uncle Frank lifted his eyes from a nondescript spot in the corner of the room.

"Nope, not going back, no barn, no place for my tractor."

"What if we stop by the farm, run the tractor around the field for a bit? Then we'll take you back."

Mrs. Eisenburger dug in her heels. "After we find his mother's still."

"We? You're coming along?"

"I might be the most qualified person there is for this assignment. You don't expect me to babysit the library while you delve into our local history. I'm not running daycare for adults here."

She spread an assortment of pamphlets, papers, and books across the table. I pulled up a chair. The first book she shoved in front of me was Laura Ingalls Wilder's *Farmer Boy*, which she explained was the second book of the *Little House on the Prairie* series. As she read in her animated librarian voice, the story of Alice and Almanzo foraging the hillside for teaberries came to life. She definitely has my attention with the description of the mother mixing the thick green leaves with whiskey to make wintergreen flavoring for cakes and cookies.

"Wintergreen, that's chewing gum, isn't it?" I asked.

"Wintergreen, teaberry, checkerberry, all the same thing," she replied without missing a beat. "A small bush, white bell-shaped flowers, little red berries, fragrant leaves."

Uncle Frank's eyes returned from a round trip to the vacant corner. "I was there when my mother drove us up a gate road into the hills. We spent our afternoons combing the meadow for teaberries. She mixed her berries with her homemade vodka and sold the extract at the market. Her teaberry still, we have to find it before it disappears."

"What if we—?"

Mrs. Eisenburger finished my sentence, "—find the still? Good idea!"

I was trapped between a librarian with a folklorist agenda and a mentally faltering uncle in whose brain bits and pieces of our family lore slowly faded away.

While I reread the *Farmer Boy* passage from a new perspective, Mrs. Eisenburger stopped by the microfiche reader and scoped a few sheets of paper from the hopper. She sat down beside me, reading from a turn of the century advertisement offering teaberry extract to counter inflammation.

Uncle Frank continued his time-traveling monologue. "She boiled the leaves, condensed the steam through a coil, and collected the oil in a canning jar."

His eyes made another round trip to the corner of the room. "We were all she had. She fed us during the Depression. After my dad died in '34, the neighbors talked about us in the third person, the Widow Guthrie, alone in the world with two small children."

As I processed my distant grandmother, I came to see a younger version of Uncle Frank, the boy before he became parts manager at the Ford dealer, toastmaster at several dozen weddings, auctioneer at the Rotary Charity Benefit.

Mrs. Eisenburger kicked my shin under the table. "Enough talk, time to act."

She escorted us to the parking lot and secured Uncle Frank into his seatbelt as a mother sends her child off to kindergarten. She walked around to my side, leaned in the window, "Ready for an adventure?"

Before I could answer, a police car pulled up beside us. Corporal Eisenburger leaned out the window. "Hope to see you again, Guthrie, but next time leave your delivery van at home."

Frank smiled, recognizing the gestures for a joke, but with no memory of the van. The neurons still functioning in his brain focused on a long-lost teaberry still. Mrs. Eisenburger slipped into the backseat with her bottomless black pocketbook.

"Where exactly are we headed?" I asked, tapping my fingers on the steering wheel, waiting politely for instructions. I didn't have to wait long.

Before she could answer, Uncle Frank interrupted with another litany. "Now I remember. The still was beside a small stream. There was a large chestnut tree lying dead on the hillside. Momma trimmed the branches to stoke the fire into a bed of coals. There was a swamp down the hill from us. We parked the van on the edge and walked in."

Mrs. Eisenburger listened intently before speaking. "I'd considered Fork Run or Savage River, but now maybe Cranesville near the swamp."

She reached into the recesses of her pocketbook and extracted a hand-drawn map. "Left onto Fourth Street, left again on Bankers Road, continue onto Herrington Manor Road, slight left onto Cranesville Road, then Burnside Camp Road to Cranesville Swamp."

Uncle Frank rambled on. "No place for my tractor, not going back, nope, never."

Mrs. Eisenburger reassured him. "You're not going back, not this afternoon anyway, not if I can help it."

I glanced at my watch, "We'll drive as long as you like."

She stiffened her lips with a slight Teutonic edge worthy of her last name, "We're not driving around aimlessly. I know exactly where we're headed. We'll find the still. It's there. I know it."

She was wrong. We drove around for the next two hours, back and forth on Sang Run Road, in and out of West Virginia, a loop around Lodestone up to Fork Run, and up and down Cranesville Road. She barked instructions from the notes and maps she'd spread across the backseat. Finally, just across the state line, Uncle Frank bolted upright. "The dirt road beyond the stop sign, left up the hill."

Following his directions, I steered onto a gravel road along the bluff overlooking the swamp. Mrs. Eisenburger supervised as I opened and closed the periodic gates along the way, a difficult maneuver stepping across slippery cattle guards. As we inched along, she craned her neck out the rear window to verify the latch was securely fastened. I, on the other hand, was more concerned about the clearance of my sedan over the ruts and potholes as well as the prospect of backing out several hundred yards if there was no turnaround.

All the while, Uncle Frank continued his time travels in and out of the 1930s. "We might be close. Mom carried a basket for the leaves and a jar for the berries. A bridge across a stream, we played there. One day the still was gone, nothing left but the boiler, the coil, her jars, her stash, gone."

The road twisted along the drive of an abandoned country club and past a stand of hemlock. When we reached the knoll of the hill, Mrs. Eisenburger issued another command. "Stop, pull over here."

She turned as she slid out of the car. "Come on, let's go."

Uncle Frank stayed behind, staring absently into the hemlock. The fog of senility descended once again. I dutifully followed her, but not before removing my keys from the ignition. Twenty or thirty yards along the ridge, she stood beside a small bush, knowingly sniffing a leaf before handing it to me. "Definitely teaberry."

I rolled the leaf between my fingers, a familiar scent covering my skin, like chewing gum without the mint. She confirmed her identification. "A small bush, white bell-shaped flowers, little red berries, fragrant leaves."

Back in the car, we continued past a collapsed barn covered with ivy and rolled to a stop where a small stream had eroded the hillside, including what remained of the road. Uncle Frank rolled out of his car seat and followed a deer trail downhill to a creek. Minutes later we found him on the bank leaning up against a fallen chestnut. Mrs. Eisenburger waded into the shallow water and pried a rusted metal roof from a collapsed shed. Soon we three stood ankle-deep in the current, navigating slick moss-covered stones, pulling objects from the water: copper tubing, canning jars, a fire chamber, and a broken caldron.

"Whose land is this?" I asked.

She looked up. "Ours for the afternoon, then they can have it back."

"But this stuff doesn't belong to us."

"It's been on the bottom of the creek for fifty years."

"Do you think we have the right spot, the right still?"

"Doesn't matter, we found what we came for."

Maybe it was my grandmother's still, maybe a local gin mill, but that day it belonged to us. She reached into the wreckage and presented Uncle Frank with an ancient whiskey bottle. "You'll need a souvenir. Pay attention to the bubbles in the amber glass, the heavy mold seam, and the bald eagle embossed on the front. Remember your mother. Remember us."

For me she selected a weathervane. "For you, for being a good sport, St. George and the Dragon to protect you for the rest of your life."

She pulled her camera from her pocketbook. Contorting her body from angle to angle as the shutter flickered, she snapped photo after photo: me and Uncle Frank in front of the still, close ups of the whiskey bottle and the weathervane, archeological shots of the still and creek bottom.

On the way home, she directed us to an Amish roadside stand where we filled our basket with teaberry jam for me and

Uncle Frank and a brick of white chocolate for Aunt Diane. Despite her protests, I treated Mrs. Eisenburger to several jars of apple butter and orange marmalade.

"Now what?" I asked when we returned to the library parking lot.

She kissed me on the forehead. "I guess you'll have to take him back."

"You're okay with that?"

"Yes."

The next morning, we were all back, Mrs. Eisenburger at the library babysitting wayward octogenarians, Uncle Frank presiding over senile Rotarians at the assisted-living breakfast table, and me on my patio sipping Trader Joe's Columbian and spreading teaberry jam on shortbread biscuits. Before I called my answering service to check in for the day, I ceremoniously placed my St. George weathervane over the garden shed to guard against hedgehogs, moles, squash bugs, and dragons. To this day, I have yet to lose a single pumpkin to fire-breathing dragons.

A Shotgun Wedding

Amy was eight-and-a-half months pregnant the Saturday we married. As her family constantly reminded her, she was the second daughter of the longtime rector of the Washington Street Episcopal Church, blue-blooded as they come. For months her parents had lobbied for a proper church wedding. Nudging didn't work. Neither did cajoling, bribing, or threatening. What the parishioners might think was of little concern to her. Early in our relationship I made it a point never to get between Amy and her father.

We spent the morning tucked away in our Annapolis apartment, ready for the final assault. I piddled in the kitchen, cleaning up the dinner dishes from the previous evening, intermittently sipping a cup of lukewarm coffee and leafing through the newspaper on the counter. Amy retreated upstairs to her art studio in the loft. She spoke with her mother on the phone, the receiver cradled under her chin. Her paintbrush floated over her canvas as she spoke. I recognize the glint in her eye when she contemplates an eddy swirling around a sandbar, a waterspout roping up into the clouds, a silver streak where the osprey dives into a school of fish. I hear the rasp of her putty knife as she chops mounds of violet and lavender on her palette, the staccato peck as she bounces peaks of hot pink into the slurry. I feel the rush when she splatters a peacock sunset across the twilight. Amy's evening skies are definitely not etherized upon the table.

I heard only her end of the phone call. "Mom, we'll figure it out. We're adults, twenty-four-year-old unmarried adults. I don't care what other people think. My father the rector won't have a kitten. It's biologically impossible. No, I didn't spend too many unsupervised, adolescent evenings upstairs in the rectory reading *Lady Chatterley's Lover* while he hosted the church elders in the parlor below."

At 9:30 a.m. the doorbell rang.

"Go away," I shouted from my recliner.

A few minutes later it rang again.

"Get that!" Amy yelled down the stairs. "I'm on the phone."

I leaned out the window and shouted, "Who is it?"

"Your darling sister Susan."

"Did Dad send you?" I asked.

"Will you let me in or not?"

"Not until you tell me if Dad sent you."

"He's out in the car."

"Any others?"

She rang the doorbell again. "Let me in. It's starting to rain."

"Not until you tell me how many others."

"Me and Dad."

"Can we meet for lunch?" I asked. "The diner at noon?"

"We'll be there."

I watched from the living room window as they drove away, then retreated to the recliner in my alcove to collect my thoughts. Amy's phone conversation with her mother raged in the loft above. "This is my baby. I'll tend to the matter myself. No, we won't marginalize the scandal with a discreet ceremony in an out-of-the-way chapel. I don't want a big church wedding like my sisters."

When I heard her coming down the stairs, I scurried from the recliner back to the kitchen where I pretended to be wiping the counter, wondering what to say. She spoke first, "Who was at the door?"

"Susan. She wants to talk, the diner at noon."

"Finally, somebody sane, normal."

"You're okay with that?"

"I'm famished. This baby is hungry."

I'd always thought my family was abnormal, but here we were, a few inches up the normality spectrum from the rector himself.

She wasn't finished. "Can I borrow your Terrapins sweatshirt? I seem to have outgrown my jogging suit."

Susan and Dad were waiting in the diner parking lot. We followed them inside. The receptionist greeted us at her station and escorted us through the narrow dining room to a long table in the rear. "Your party's in the back."

"You lied to me," I scolded Susan. "You said there weren't any others."

"In the car. I said Dad was the only one in the car."

"How many other others are there?"

"Rose and Pam."

"That's all? Just Amy's sisters?"

"Except for Rose's two-year-old April, that's it for now."

"For now?"

Pam and Rose with April in tow met us halfway across the dining room, swarming all over Amy's belly. Pam was dressed in her work clothes, cotton slacks and a white V-neck under a tan cardigan, Rose in jeans and a tie-dye Grateful Dead T-shirt, little April still in her pajamas. Obviously, Rose had snatched her from her bed when she received Pam's phone call about our rapidly developing shotgun wedding.

"Listen, I can hear the heartbeat," Pam said with her ear to Amy's navel.

"And here, I felt a kick," said Rose. "The baby has dropped."

Amy scooted around the table and took a seat between Dad and me to escape the barrage from her sisters.

"I don't see why you can't get married before the baby comes and make Mom happy," said Rose.

"It won't make any difference in the long run. You've been together since high school," Pam agreed. "Consider how this looks to our parents."

"This is my body and my baby, nothing to do with the Episcopal Church."

I should have kept my mouth shut, but I didn't. "Hypothetically, suppose we go for a quick wedding. What's the timeline?"

Pam smoothed her napkin out on the table with the side of a pencil and began to scribble. "Okay, the hypothetical timeline."

"The baby's dropped," Rose reminded her sister. "We don't have much time."

Pam licked the pencil lead as if that might improve her concentration. "We'll schedule around that."

"I only look like I'll explode," Amy said. "We have a couple more days."

"That's why we're here," Rose burst in. "Can you listen for a change?"

"I am listening. Let's say I go along with this. How do we make it work?"

"We're here. Mom and Dad are on their way."

"I know. Mom's called me three times so far this morning. Her last call was from a payphone at a rest stop on Route 40 somewhere west of Frederick."

Pam continued to scribble on her napkin. "Amy and Dave swing by the courthouse for a license. Meanwhile Rose and I find a chapel somewhere."

"There's a problem with the license," Amy said. "The courthouse is closed Saturdays."

"What about Dad?" Rose asked. "He can open doors."

As if on cue, a new group appeared at the reception. My father-in-law-to-be Walter James knew how to make an entrance. He waved to the other restaurant patrons as he loped across the floor. My mother-in-law-to-be Sheila James, my Uncle Robbie, and my Aunt Beth followed in single file. Along the way Walter shared the story of their day in a rambling conversation with the receptionist.

"We always brunch at the South Mountain Inn, but today we missed the turn onto Alternate 40 in Hagerstown. Beth suggested the Dutch's Daughter in Frederick."

"The Dutch's Daughter serves excellent crab quiche," Sheila added. "But Walter wouldn't give up on South Mountain. He backtracked on the National Pike in Frederick and took the wrong exit onto 340 toward West Virginia."

"A slight navigation error," Walter explained.

"Did you ever eat?" the waiter asked.

"We found a hot dog machine at the Sheetz Qwik Shopper in Brunswick," Uncle Robbie explained.

"A computerized hot dog machine," Walter added.

"But we're still hungry," Aunt Beth said.

"We can remedy that," the waiter said. "Maybe start with a little orange juice and a club sandwich."

Sheila glanced at her wristwatch to confirm the time. "Make mine a mimosa."

Walter nodded his approval. "I take mine with a double-shot of bourbon."

Pam slapped her hands on the table, "A pitcher of mimosas with highball glasses and one Shirley Temple in a plastic cup, a side of bourbon for the old man."

"That's settled," Walter announced before turning to Amy and adjusting his clerical collar into High Episcopal. "What's this about no wedding?"

The past five months found Amy locked in a parental conflict with her father. In his opinion (and I quote), "We Jameses don't have children out of wedlock, out of the question, not on my watch."

Amy stood firm, "Your watch, my baby."

Meanwhile Sheila probed me for any weakness. "What would your mother think?"

Aunt Beth chimed in with her opinion before I could answer, "I'm glad she's not here to see this."

I knew what my mother would say. "McNichols don't have babies out of wedlock, either."

Amy kicked me under the table to steer my answer in the right direction. "She'd be thrilled with her first grandchild, hospital first, chapel later."

"Don't just sit there. Tell us what you feel," Sheila said, ignoring my answer.

My most visceral feeling was how we'd manage to remove an eight-pound baby in a watermelon-sized cocoon from Amy's protruding belly. Before I could vocalize the thought, Amy kicked me again. I backed her with the best words I could muster. "I'm in this for the short term and the long term."

"That doesn't mean anything," Aunt Beth said.

"You're just as stubborn as Amy," Sheila snapped.

She was wrong there. No one was as stubborn as Amy when she dug in her heels.

I was outnumbered and outgunned, a twenty-four-year-old male confronting my future mother-in-law eight-and-a-half unmarried months after I knocked up her daughter.

"Out with it," Aunt Beth demanded.

Amy answered for me. "He's a lucky boy, my lover, the father of my child."

"The father of your illegitimate child."

"Not illegitimate yet," Pam corrected. "We have two days."

"What about the wedding?" Walter asked her.

Rose came to the rescue. "She said she'd listen. We're working on hypothetical."

"What can I do to move things along?"

"We have you penciled in for the license and the chapel," Pam said.

"I can make a few phone calls."

"The courthouse is closed," Amy reminded him.

Walter had arrived prepared. "I know the rector at St. Bartholomew's. We can use his chapel. His brother is a judge with the circuit court. He can help with the license."

"I bet he can pull a license out of his ass," Susan whispered under her breath.

Amy poached a potato from my lunch platter. "I give up. I'll do it," she conceded, throwing her arms into the air. "But no one gives me away."

Walter acquiesced, nodding his most reverend benediction. Shelia swallowed hard but kept silent. Pam stuffed the timeline recorded on her napkin into her pocketbook and kept silent. We had a meeting of minds. Off to the chapel.

Word of the wedding spread quickly. When we arrived at the church, a dozen friends and family members milled around in the shade of the oak grove between the old stone church and the cemetery. Cars trickled into the church parking lot all afternoon About 3:00 p.m. the St. Bartholomew rector and his brother, the circuit court judge, arrived in a Mercedes Coupe with a marriage license and the keys to the chapel. When a passenger van from the retirement community arrived, an attendant wheeled Grandma Guthrie into the chapel. We were ready.

Even though the circumstances were bizarre, the service was by the book, the Episcopal Book of Common Prayer, which Walter kept at the ready in his hip pocket. Once everyone was seated, he adjusted his clerical collar and began to read. "In the presence of God, Father, Son and Holy Spirit, we have come together to witness the marriage of Amy and Dave, to pray for God's blessing on them, to share their joy and to celebrate their love."

Amy's contractions began as her father rambled into "They will each give their consent to the other and make solemn vows, and in token of this they will each give and receive a ring."

We didn't have rings. Nevertheless, Rose's daughter April filled the role of ring bearer as gracefully as any ringless, unrehearsed toddler could. Susan joined Amy's sisters Rose and Pam as bridesmaids. Dad filled in dutifully as my best man.

"Who gives this woman?" Walter said, departing from Amy's script.

"I do," Amy assured everyone. "I give myself to my buddy."

"Do you, Dave McNichol, take this woman—"

"He's not taking anything. I'm giving myself away. He's a lucky boy."

After the ceremony, a makeshift tailgate reception formed in the parking lot. Friends we'd not seen since my mother's funeral arrived with platters of eggplant casserole, smoked trout, and every imaginable variety of pasta salad. Stragglers continued to arrive throughout the afternoon. My boss Dick Hogan and his brother arrived in his pickup with a barbecue trailer in tow. Amy's college roommate and the other members of the Black-Eyed Susan String Band drove up from their home base in St. Mary's County.

We celebrated into the evening, guests one by one offering toasts between Amy's contractions. Cheers erupted after each toast and each series of contractions. After an endless round of toasts to family, friendship, pregnancy, babies, and crazy weddings, Uncle Robbie stood and took the microphone. "Several years ago, my sister Sandy, Burt's mother, this baby's grandmother, passed away. Not a day goes by that her last words do not reverberate, 'I won't be there to see my grandchildren. Watch over them. Keep them safe.' Last night she appeared once again in my dreams. 'Carry me with you tomorrow that I may bless my children, my grandchild.'"

He handed me the microphone and returned to his seat. "Your turn. Let your mother in."

I felt Mom's presence. I shared her words with the wedding guests. "My mother's last words to me were simple and direct, 'Marry her. You can't do any better. You know that, don't you?'"

"You're a lucky boy," Susan shouted for the final toast of the evening.

Shortly after 7:00 p.m., the wedding party formed a ragtag convoy of Fords and Buicks. We all headed to the Hospital Center. Staff quickly escorted us to the birthing suite, an operating room disguised as a bedroom and an outer waiting room with sofas and a kitchenette. Throughout the night, I was back and forth between the two rooms. Amy and her two sister-coaches worked in unison as the baby inched down her birth canal.

Just before dawn I fell asleep in an easy chair in the waiting room. The next thing I remember was Amy's mother Sheila, bouncing through the room, "Wake up. She's darling. Come see. She's ours."

She grabbed my hand and dragged me to the bedroom where Amy lay with our infant daughter Rachael in her arms. She lifted the slithery, slimy redhead from Amy's arms and placed her in mine. "Welcome to the family," she said in her most High Episcopal. I assumed she meant both me and Rachael.

Amy smiled and said nothing. It had been a long day.

A Single Father

3:10 a.m. The room is dark. Mehitabel[†] rocks side to side in an autistic trance, kneads her front paws into the cotton cord of the throw rug. Her tail snakes haltingly, randomly through the darkness, moving with her eyes. The leap center in her frontal lobes runs through several thousand calculations to determine the correct tail position and thrust vector for several destinations in the room.

Gradually, imperceptibly, her posture morphs from dingy barn cat to the tense longitude of a leaper. Freezing into a stance, she stares intensely at the bed board, gauging the distance. For a few seconds, the invisible clock in her animal brain completes the sweepings of minute and second hands. The primeval countdown proceeds. The room is still but for the flurry in her leap control center, the wildness behind motionless eyes. Then the unmistakable quiver of a front paw shaking free from the loose threads of the rug. Her tail snaps back. She springs. Her cocked body releases itself into motion.

3:11 a.m. The room is dark. A dreamer glides aimlessly through convoluted pathways of the human brain asleep in the bed, archiving thoughts, words, inflections, sights, sounds, and fragrances of the day. This was an easy task in the old days before John McDowell's wife left him with two daughters, an eight-year-old and a four-year-old. When its task was complete, the dreamer wandered the neurons as a caretaker wanders garden paths, touching stones, inhaling deeply, listening, sighing. Back then the memories were pleasant, hiking the Appalachian Trail, fishing on the Outer Banks, soft-shelled crabs at Happy Harbor.

Two years later the dreamer catalogues a prototypical single-father nightmare. John sits in his cubicle at a no-name federal agency in the District of Columbia, a sixty-minute train ride from his home in western Maryland. He glances at his watch, midafternoon, time for Sykes Landing Elementary to load its students into bright yellow buses and send them home. He reaches for his telephone, but the buttons fall off in his hand. His boss walks by and stuffs unfinished budget reports into his inbox. He can't read his train schedule because the letters are smeared with coffee stains. John is miles and hours away from his family.

3:12 a.m. John is startled awake in the predawn by the hiss of the throw rug across the hard-polished floor. He emerges from his slumber to confront an embarrassed barn cat. Mehitabel hangs precariously from the bed board, her claws too tangled in the ancient threads of Grandmother Eisenberger's double wedding band quilt to fall gracefully to the floor.

John leans up from his sleep and gropes through the darkness for the foot board and then along the foot board for the imperiled cat. One hand lifts Mehitabel beneath her belly while the other works to free her claws from the entanglement. Within a few seconds John lies asleep again in the giant, soft bed. Mehitabel sleeps peacefully at his side. There's no dreamer in her pea brain to archive the embarrassing moment.

3:28 a.m. The dreamer encounters a new variation of the nightmare. The previous afternoon at the office when John returned from coffee with his coworkers, he found a note on his desk, a short note devoid of meaning. "Call Mrs. Iverson at Sykes Landing Elementary about your daughter Denise." The note is forty-five minutes old.

One of the evolutionary adaptations of the McDowell clan is the ability of mature females past childbearing age to assist with the care and nurture of their grandchildren while their sons and daughters venture out to earn a living. John instinctively reached for his phone to call his mother. He whined into the telephone. "Mom! What about this note? I have to call the school."

"It's okay, dear. Cathleen took care of it."

His mother speaks in short sentences with the rhythm of a reassuring heartbeat. "There, there, Sonny. Try to relax."

He didn't want to relax. He wanted to know about the note. Then he'd make up his own mind whether he should relax.

"What did Cathleen take care of? What did they want?"

"Denise owed the library $4.53 in overdue fines. She couldn't sign up for a field trip to the Brunswick Railroad Museum until they were paid."

John resents the arrogance of Mrs. Iverson, who wields the power to compel a parent to leave work and drive across the countryside with $4.53. He fumbled around in his wallet and extracted a five-dollar bill. His mother didn't have to pay the fine. He's good for it. He conjured the image of his older daughter Cathleen parading down the hall of the elementary school in her best imitation of an adult and handing the envelope to Mrs. Iverson. He could picture the crisp, white envelope reading "Mrs. Iverson" in his mother's pristine calligraphy.

"Mom! I'll be home on the first train. I'll stop by the school in time to talk to somebody."

"That's not necessary. We took care of it. I can chaperone Denise's first grade class on the field trip."

The dreamer shakes its head. It wishes it could help, but that's not its job. Its job is to archive memories. It's not certified to change anything.

3:42 a.m. John is startled from his sleep by the snap of the light switch in the hall. Harsh, yellow light gushes out of the hallway into his bedroom. He leans up from the bed sheets into dark, yellow shapes. He watches Denise inch past the bedroom door and disappear into the bathroom. A few minutes later, she inches back down the hall. There's another spring-gun snap as the light goes out.

4:05 a.m. John lies in bed, stares at the ceiling to contemplate his situation. His is a familiar story. A young man and a young woman are married in 1969. They move to Arlington, Virginia, where he works in the city. She stays home with children and churns out unpublished novels. The years pass. She experiences the emptiness of a career husband, ever-present children, bland Arlington, and harsh rejection slips. When she can't take any more, she runs off with her lover to live in an efficiency apartment in Adams Morgan where there's no pressure and no pretense.

John suffers under the stress of bedwetting daughters, no-show babysitters, and an absent wife. He moves his dwindling family back home to western Maryland where he can be close to his mother. Here he can ride the commuter train to work in Washington. He buys an old Sears mail-order house with a wrap-around front porch, loud 1920s' light switches, bare 1950s' yellow light bulbs, no curtains, and no carpeting. He works on the bedwetting. Soon Cathleen gets up every morning at four to pee. Denise is down to three or four accidents a week.

5:15 a.m. John wakes up as close as he'll ever get to an epiphany. He rolls out of bed to check Denise's overstuffed book bag. Beneath a half-eaten peanut butter sandwich and a moldy snack cake, he finds a ten-day old note from Mrs. Iverson asking him to chaperone the first graders to the railroad museum.

He digs deeper into the book bag to find four overdue book notices. Why didn't anybody tell him to rummage through his kids' book bags for field trips and library fines? He pounds his head on the bed board. How could he have been so naïve?

5:20 a.m. Mehitabel isn't worried about anything except the throw rug. How is a cat to catapult herself into the air without firm footing? The humans should carpet the entire place. That would eliminate her traction problems. Then she could sharpen her claws anywhere she happened to be standing.

5:55 a.m. John lifts his head from the pillow and turns his eyes to the night stand, concentrating intensely to bring the alarm clock into focus. He winces from his recurring nightmare. He's at the office, ready to quit for the day when his manager dumps another assignment on his desk. He glances at his watch, then at the train schedule taped to the wall. The last train leaves at 7:15 p.m. He won't be home until 8:30 p.m. If he misses the train, the cab ride home is $75. He's miles and hours from his family.

6:23 a.m. Cathleen stands at the foot of the stairs yelling. "Denise, get your derriere in gear. I'm headed out for the newspaper. When I get back, I'd better not find you in bed!"

She wears her father's wool hunting socks and her mother's flannel nightgown. She has one hand on the corner post of the banister and the other on her hip. "Do you have any idea what time it is? Almost 6:30. Daddy has to be on the train by 7:30. I want you in and out of the bathroom in ten minutes. Grandma will pick you up for the field trip. Be dressed and ready. And stay away from the thermostat. It's not to be set above sixty-five. I don't care if you have your mother's circulation. You're not the one paying the oil bills."

She slides across the hard, waxed floor in her stocking feet as she heads into the kitchen. There, in a few quick, practiced movements, she sets a pot of coffee percolating and pitches a package of sticky buns into the oven. She hustles back into Denise's room to check for wet sheets.

7:30 a.m. John McDowell steers his Ford Falcon down his serpentine driveway on the way to the train station. He instinctively checks his briefcase on the front passenger seat for his corned-beef sandwich, the management summary report for a 10 a.m. staff meeting, the *Washington Post*, and his coffee thermos. At the bottom of the hill, he passes his mother's Buick Roadmaster turning into the driveway to pick up Denise for the field trip to the railroad museum. She waves a reassuring wave to John. He waves back as he heads into the District for another day at the office.

8:15 a.m. Mehitabel's ears snap up. The sound is unmistakable, the pitter-patter of mouse feet in the pantry. In one quick motion she leaps from the bed, races down the hall, and bursts into the kitchen where she nails the obnoxious rodent gnawing his way into a box of corn flakes. Meticulously she positions the half-eaten carcass on the counter beside the toaster. Having earned her lodging for the day, she returns to the bedroom to continue her snooze. She purrs softly, assured that the McDowell family is delighted to possess such an accomplished trophy cat.

10:00 a.m. Grandmother McDowell is a mainstay of the Brunswick Railroad Museum. Her grandfather was an engineer for the B&O Railroad and one of the last men who knew steam engines inside and out. When she slips into a parking place on Potomac Street in front of the museum, all four doors of her car pop open to eject a torrent of hyperactive first graders. She follows them with a tray of fudge brownies. Once inside, she leads the children around the model railroad, where she points out the B&O passenger line between Union Station in Washington and the Brunswick railyards, the Brunswick roundhouse, the Potomac River, and the C&O canal. The first graders are less fascinated with the Victorian costumes and the medical history exhibits. The fudge brownies are a big hit, maybe a bit too much sugar for midmorning.

3:00 p.m. Mrs. Iverson's low voice blares over the loudspeaker in the parking lot outside Sykes Landing Elementary. One by one she dispatches busses to destinations in the south county: Sandy Hook, Bluff City, Sykes Landing. From her control center in the assistant principal's office, she watches as the children board their busses. She fails to notice when Denise slips behind the Sykes Landing bus and darts across the playground to the canal. Cathleen follows in a vain effort to steer her back to the parking lot. Denise prefers the tow path of the C&O canal to the confining bus ride. The walk along the canal is much faster than the bus' circuitous trip through the town.

3:15 p.m. John returns to his desk after coffee break to find another note from Mrs. Iverson. "Your daughters are missing, last seen loitering in the bus parking lot after school. They didn't board the bus, nor are they anywhere on school grounds. I'll call their grandmother. Maybe she knows something."

3:25 p.m. Cathleen sits at the lone picnic table at the Battery Bluff Roadside Park. Denise plays at the water fountain several yards away. Every so often she violates one of the tenets of the moral order as Cathleen perceives it, and Cathleen lets fly a harangue of "do's," "ought's," "else's," and "should's." Each word, each phrase, is an end in itself, a lone projectile. Each insolent mouthful is part of an ancient Presbyterian litany.

"Denise! Listen here! Put down that rock! Don't mark up those signs! What will people think? I said put down that rock! I've had it with you!"

As Cathleen speaks, word after word whines through the afternoon haze. Each staccato burst is lofted high up into the heavy afternoon air. Each word, each hasty phrase, rushes back down through the heat and haze to Denise who pays no attention whatsoever.

3:25 p.m. John sits at his desk, sipping the dregs of his cold coffee. He sets Mrs. Iverson's note down and retrieves his commuter rail schedule. If he leaves immediately, he can catch the 4:05 Martinsburg Express. He phones the Happy Panda in the Union Station eatery for Chinese carryout. He can feed his family.

4:15 p.m. The next stage in the sister's journey home involves a pitstop at their grandparents' house on Fayette Street where leftover fudge brownies await them. Several times a week, Grandma sits down with Cathleen and Denise to gather intelligence on the evolving fortunes of the family and to precipitate as many mid-course corrections to the evolution as possible. Her generation believes that individuals once married should stay married and that it's the duty of the ranking female within the extended family to preserve the ties which bind the family together. She regards Cathleen as the ranking female heiress apparent, and thus, as the one most likely to influence her wayward parents.

"Your mother? Have you heard from her?"

Cathleen answers, "She called last week."

"What did she have to say?"

"She wanted to speak to Daddy."

"And?"

"She wanted to borrow some money for a trip to Mexico with her boyfriend."

"Mexico!"

"Daddy says it's to look at old temples and smoke dope."

"It's a shame, two people giving up on each other. Come stay with us until they get back together."

"No, Daddy needs us at home."

Cathleen sits on the couch with her hands folded in her lap and her legs crossed at the knee. She nods at appropriate points in the conversation with the art and grace of a loyal but evasive understudy. The children have adjusted nicely to life on the roam. Since Cathleen makes up the few rules required for their simple, country existence, they see no need for a full-time rule maker. No one except Grandpa can live with Grandma twenty-four hours a day.

5:05 p.m. Cathleen and Denise arrive home. They retrieve the latch key from its hiding place under a fake rock in the garden and let themselves in. Denise hides several fudge brownies behind the vegetables in the refrigerator for a late-night snack. Cathleen removes the half-eaten mouse from the kitchen counter and sanitizes the locale with chlorine bleach. Mehitabel peers around the corner from the basement stairs, purring self-satisfaction.

5:55 p.m. John, Cathleen, and Denise sit at the dining room table enjoying Happy Panda carryout: a Pu Pu platter, wanton soup, fried rice, and General Tso's chicken. After dinner, John dutifully inspects Denise's bookbag for library fines and half-eaten sandwiches. John is a work in progress.

3:10 a.m. The room is dark. Mehitabel rocks side to side in an autistic trance, kneads her front paws into the cotton cord of the throw rug. Her tail snakes haltingly, randomly through the darkness, moving with her eyes. The leap center in her frontal lobes runs through several thousand calculations to determine the correct tail position and thrust vector for several destinations in the room.

Mehitabel, an alley cat, and Archy, a philosopher cockroach, were created by *New York Evening Sun* columnist Don Marquis beginning in 1916. The stories were subsequently collected into book form as *Archy and Mehitabel* (Doubleday: 1926).

Show and Tell

North Branch Elementary, room twelve, kindergarten, I was there, a three-year-old boy at my mother's side, the day my perfect sister Anne unveiled the first cloth squares of a patchwork quilt, each square snugly tucked into a saddle oxford shoe box.

A virtuoso performance, self-confidence I've yet to master, poise you'd not believe, square-shouldered, she paraded down the hall and into the classroom, her masterpiece cradled in her arms. My mother and I followed, two paces back, one pace to either side. After a brief roundtrip though the cloak room to deposit her lunch box, she confidently slid the magic box onto her desk. I stood in the corner with my mother, taking in the scene through my thick-lensed glasses.

After other students presented their lame exhibits, the usual beach pictures from Ocean City and bottle cap foot scrapers, Miss Wilkes nodded to Anne. "What do you have for us today?"

Anne stood before the class, erect and poised, her shoebox cradled in her arms. "A patchwork quilt for my family, squares from our favorite old clothes, blankets, and curtains. Memories my mom and I will stitch together."

The show began. Square one floated through the air and settled gingerly on the handicraft table. She beamed, "Cloth from my grandpa's flannel shirt, he never took it off."

Miss Wilkes, her creaky schoolmarm voice, "Not even for the wash?"

Another square aligned itself daintily beside the first, a flour sack from our grandpa's gristmill. Panel after panel floated from the magic box, a needlepoint from our Aunt Jane's sewing room, my Mickey Mouse T-shirt from the ragbag, a swatch from her baby blanket. When the craft table was full, Anne stepped back for all to see. Miss Wilkes, cheerleader to generations, led the applause. Even the boys in the back row stood and peered.

Anne Guthrie, valedictorian at Allegany High School, cum laude at Johns Hopkins, I was there at her humble beginning, the day she aced show-and-tell at North Branch Elementary.

Two years later when I arrived for show-and-tell, it wasn't smiles that filled the room. My disastrous presentation landed me in the school reception sitting on a cold, metal folding chair while my classmates enjoyed afternoon recess in the playground. Miss Wilkes trailed her finger down the emergency contacts to our home phone number. "Mrs. Guthrie, can you pick up your son Steve?"

"Who's this?" Mom asked.

"Miss Wilkes from the elementary school."

"Steve? Is he hurt? What happened?"

"No, but there's a problem. Your son brought a box of bees to school."

"Bees?"

"That's what I said, bees."

"That's not possible. How can a five-year-old boy carry bees across town on the school bus?"

"Apparently your son is a capable young man."

"Was anyone stung?"

"No, but he sure emptied the classroom."

Mid-afternoon found Miss Wilkes in the parking lot with me and the bees. Mom pulled up in her station wagon. "I'm sorry. This won't happen again."

She turned to me. "Will it?"

"With the bees?"

"Not with anything else."

"We don't want to stifle the boy's creativity, do we?" Miss Wilkes added.

The rhetorical question hung in the air unanswered. Mom wasn't in a rhetorical mood.

On the way home, when I expected Mom's appropriate / inappropriate lecture, she couldn't resist the obvious question, "How did you get the bees into the box?"

"At night, Dad told me they sleep at night. I slipped a rack into a cookie tin."

Her lecture stewed in her head while we rode up the hillside in silence. She exploded when she steered off the road onto our long, winding driveway. "What were you thinking?"

"Dad said they sleep at night."

"It's not night now, is it?"

"Last night it was."

When we pulled into the carport, Mom left me alone in the car with the motor running. I waited a few minutes for her return, then turned the ignition key to the off position and followed her into the house.

"What now?" I asked when I found her in the kitchen.

"I'll see to dinner. You work on the story you're going to tell your father."

"Can't you just paddle me?"

"That would be too easy."

Mom was wrong. My conversation with Dad wasn't as painful as I'd anticipated, just a sprinkling of have-you-lost-your-mind and what-will-the-neighbors-think. My story traced a disastrous day from a 5:00 a.m. visit to the beehives to stashing the bee-laden cookie tin in my bookbag to the bumpy school bus ride to me dropping a tray of angry bees in front of my show-and-tell audience.

Dad struggled to maintain a straight face as I described the mayhem in the classroom. His lecture ended with a fatherly let-the-punishment-fit-the-crime, a letter of apology to Miss Wilkes and my classmates. Anne helped me with the note, replacing beekeeping details with sincerity and remorse.

My story improved markedly with age as it wormed its way into the family lore. It popped up randomly at wedding toasts and funeral recollections. I credit Anne with some of the embellishments including Miss Wilkes' gushy kindergarten language and Dad's facial expression during his have-you-lost-your-mind lecture.

Cousins

The phone rang after midnight. Bleary-eyed, I reached to answer it over my snoring, unemployed boyfriend. My cousin Rachael, hysterical, sobbed from the receiver, "Allison, is that you?"

"Who is this? Rachael?"

"I can't believe it, horrible."

"Catch your breath. What's wrong."

"An accident, Polish Mountain in an ice storm. They skidded off the road."

"Who?"

"Mom and Dad."

"Uncle Bill? Aunt Lois?"

"Gone."

"What? How?"

"Seventy-five degrees and sunny when they left Annapolis in the morning, sleet when they reached the top of Polish Mountain forty miles short of Cumberland. One of his toys did them in, His sole request from his father's estate, his Buick Roadmaster, the one with the chrome portholes."

"I'm on my way. Where are you?"

"Annapolis, the bungalow, with their dogs. They asked me to check on them while they were going."

"No, stay put. I'll be there. What time is it?"

"I'm good for now. Come early tomorrow. I can't take another accident. I need you alive."

When I arrived in the morning, Rachael and two dogs lay asleep on the living room floor. She'd retrieved her mother's watercolor of the Roadmaster from its spot over the mantel and leaned it against the couch. She rose onto her elbows and wiped the tears from her eyes. "I can't believe they're gone. I talked to her yesterday before they left for the mountains. They planned a hike in Dolly Sods. She loved it there."

I held her in my arms until she fell asleep, then lay awake for hours, listening to her quiet snooze, petting the dogs, wondering, "What now?"

Family members arrived at the house, one by one throughout the afternoon, all chattering, none listening. "We need a plan… No, we don't…What about the service? Don't forget their out-of-town friends. They can't drop everything…What about the funeral home? We need a plan…No, we don't."

Rachael's sister Tracy arrived in tears, moaning through the lisp she'd inherited from her mother, years of speech therapy down the tubes, "God! No! How?"

She drove through the night, home from her senior year at Tulane in New Orleans. "How can this be? Yesterday on the phone she said they'd be down for Mardi Gras, ready to party. And now? Nothing."

My sister Jo, up from her Richmond apartment, launched into a digression on the dogs. No one addressed the catastrophe directly. Each preferred to dance on the periphery.

"The dogs, we can't leave them here…They stay together. I'll take them…No, I have a bigger yard. They like to be outside."

Neighbors, one by one, shuffled through for a quick condolence and an offering of meatloaf or lasagna. Despite the overflowing refrigerator and coolers stacked in the mudroom, we ultimately sat down on the deck for the Chinese carryout Jo grabbed on her way into town. She spread the paper boxes across the coffee table.

"Serious comfort food," she proclaimed.

No one argued.

After dinner we gathered around the dining room table for an adult conversation that ranged from the house to the last will and testament to the memorial service to the obituary to the funeral home. Again chatter chatter chatter: "I'll call the funeral home in the morning...What about their house? Leave everything the way it is...Let the girls handle that. We'll see how it goes...See how it goes? You can't just let things go...Yes, they can. It's their house...I say we need a plan...I say we don't." On and on, round and round, sisters, mothers, daughters, words, words, words.

◂ ◂ ◂ ◂

Saturday afternoon, 2:00 p.m., a dark day at St. Bartholomew Episcopal Church outside Annapolis, a dark day but harmony you'd not believe, proper acoustics for four cousins, four voices a cappella. Square shouldered, erect, we glided from the family pew and slid into the choir loft. We stood in silence, gazing into the nave, standing room only for friends, family, acquaintances, neighbors. Rachael raised a tuning fork, held it high above her head until the conversations among the mourners subsided. A gentle stroke on metal prongs and our voices spilled through the sanctuary, Uncle Bill's favorite hymn, "Ezekiel Saw the Wheel."

No one questioned why this of all hymns might be his favorite. His life was anything but religious. His taste in music bordered on an ill-defined crossover between yesterday's and tomorrow's preferences, between what he said he liked and what he liked. But once, out of the blue at a Sweet Honey in the Rock concert in Frederick, he went on record. "When I die, I want that spiritual at my service."

A last request is a last request. The song took flight.

The little wheel run by faith,

the big wheel run by the grace of God.

Rachael cued us each in turn, word by word, verse by verse, on and on, round and round, four cousins, a cappella. Gradually, perceptibly, the spirit spread through the sanctuary. Voices of friends and family joined together. Harmony and rhythm took a backseat to spontaneity and improvisation. When the song ran its course, Rachael brought us to a close with sweeping hands and a tuning fork baton. The last notes floated in fifths and thirds through the roof beams.

One by one we filed from the choir loft, hugging and kissing our way to the family pew. My mother Rose squeezed my hand when I passed, pulled me down for a kiss on the forehead. She came alive through all my senses. Her lips mouthed the words of the hymn, her lavender perfume, my hand tight in hers, my kiss on her salty cheek, her heartbeat against my chest when she hugged me. Her high voice dropped to contralto. "We're here. We're safe."

Without releasing me, she pulled Jo into the embrace and slicked her unkempt cowlick over her bangs. Jo jerked her head back with a move she perfected when she was three years old. The cowlick popped back to its defiant position.

"That's the way I like it."

"She's fine, Mom," I interceded.

My cousin Tracy lifted the program from her lap and ran her finger down the page. "I believe we're stuck somewhere near the non-existent organ interlude."

"You're right," Rachael said. "We're stuck."

She stood, smoothed the wrinkles from her skirt. I handed her the folder lying on the pew. "You forgot something."

She jerked back and stared at her papers as if an alien presence appeared before her. "No. Why?"

"The eulogy. You'll need it."

"No."

She couldn't accept the specter of her parents in the caskets. If she rejected the folder, she might somehow reject the necessity of a eulogy. Submissively she tucked her notes under her arm and made her way to the front, pausing by the caskets and running her hand along the brass handles. She wiped a smudge from the walnut grain with the tail of her scarf before ascending the steps to the lectern. Once situated, she fondled a locket hanging from her neckless. I strained to see what she found so engaging. She stared at the lifeless object, motionless for decades.

Addressing no one in particular, she began to speak. "Saint Bartholomew under the banyan tree, the son of the plowman. My mother saw the shrine in India. She traveled there when she was young."

Rachael's eyes returned to us, her cousins and sister. She scrutinized her notes, the alien sheets of paper on which she documented her mother's grace. She opened the folder, closed it again. "Monday, two days after the accident, we gathered at the bungalow, our house in Annapolis, the place we called home, all the clichés, but all the love, the tree-lined lot, the hot tub on the roof, the swinging door between the kitchen and the sunroom, the birdbath."

I leaned to Jo and whispered, "What's with Rachael? Will she ever get to her speech? She was up all night working on it."

"Too much unprocessed information," Jo replied. "That's what my therapist calls it."

"What do you think, Tracy?" I asked.

"I think it's dangerous to ask Jo what she thinks. I avoid it at all costs."

"No, I mean about the eulogy. It was beautiful when she read it to us last night."

"She'll get there. Don't worry."

"I am worried."

Rachael stared into the rafters. She stared at St. Bartholomew, gripping the rails of the lectern, speaking in a monotone. "We've lost our mother, our safe place."

Nowhere else to go, awash in her grief, she relaxed her grip on the lectern. Her eyes dropped to the pendant in her hand, then back to us. Without warning she gathered her papers and descended the stairs from the lectern. She paused in the chancel, lay her hand on the caskets, "Mom and Dad...oak planks from the barn...solid wood...may they rest in peace."

◄ ◄ ◄ ◄

The phone rang midmorning. Rachael again. "I found Dad's notebooks, boxes of photographs, papers out the wazoo, his recipe for homemade Baileys Irish Cream."

"Where? How?"

"The trunk in the attic where he kept his private papers."

"Including his madras sports jacket? The one he wore when he read Ferlinghetti's "Great Chinese Dragon"[†] poem at the Lions Club amateur night? A little long if you want my opinion."

"Come now. He needs a proper sendoff."

"I'm on my way as soon as I shake Jo awake and pour some coffee down her throat."

"Wait, there's a grocery list."

So began another day of mourning, a day when we cousins gathered to process the catastrophe on our own, to grieve without the older generation's second guesses, regrets, and alcoholic slurs.

My little sister Jo, asleep on the couch, rolled over and squinted to face me when I descended the stairs. "What's up?"

"Rachael called, something about Uncle Bill's trunk. She wants another powwow."

"When?"

"Now."

"What time is it?"

"Eleven, we slept in."

"Give me ten minutes."

"I'll clean out the car."

"Why? There's only two of us."

"We have a grocery list."

"More food? After the neighbors carpet-bombed us with lasagna and fried chicken? I don't think so."

Twenty minutes later Jo and I roamed the aisles of the Gourmet Fresh Mart in blue jeans and T-shirts, no makeup, each toting a vanilla skim latte. I read while Jo fetched: 32 ounces rye whiskey, a dozen eggs, 4 cans Eagle Brand Sweetened Condensed Milk, 4 pints of whipping cream, instant coffee, coconut extract.

The cashier scanned the items one by one across the barcode reader. "There's a story here, isn't there?"

Jo brings out the flirt in anybody. "There's always a story."

"Looks like a headache waiting to happen."

We met Tracy in the kitchen, waiting by the toaster for her bagel. "More comfort food?" she asked, pointing to my tote bag.

"Hardly."

"What then?"

"Ask Rachael. Where is she?"

"Upstairs in the loft."

We found Rachael in the roof garden under the awning, glasses scooted down her nose. She sat cross-legged on the floor, sorting through boxes of photos, mumbling.

"Best I can make out, when Granddad died, Dad cleaned out the house in Cumberland. Take a look. Every box labeled when and where: Youngstown – 1863, Sharon – 1884, Talmadge – 1902, New Bethlehem – 1918, Oberlin – 1935, Cumberland – 1986."

Dinner was dealer's choice. We delved into the refrigerator, sorting through our neighbor's latest offerings. Jo and I went straight for the meatloaf and mashed potatoes, Rachael for fried chicken, Tracy for the lobster mac and cheese. After dinner, one by one, we retired to the rooftop hot tub for Uncle Bill's final sendoff. When I rounded the corner leading to the stairs, I noticed the table full of scraps we'd left unattended. Sadie and Gwen kept a low profile from their dog beds in the corner, unable to believe their noses. Their eyes sparkled the sparkle of dogs alone with a room full of leftovers.

"What about these mutts?" I shouted upstairs to Rachael. "Want me to put the food away?"

"No, they lost their humans. Let them troll all they want."

"Where do we go from here?" I asked.

"There's only one place to go," Rachael answered.

"What's left?"

"Isn't that obvious?"

We sat silently as each contemplated the obvious, as we slipped off one by one into the rooftop hot tub. Jo, back from an extended vacation in Mexico, arrived well supplied with the Acapulco Gold she'd managed to smuggle through airport security.

Four cousins in the hot tub, what can I say, we who share our grandmother's freckles and curly red hair, all naked on the rooftop under the stars, each alone in the dark but for the others, each with her thoughts, the dreams we share.

When the time was right, after we were comfortably situated, all eyes turned to Rachael. She and Tracy disappeared behind the wet bar. Rachael returned with her father's madras sports jacket drooping over her skinny shoulders. Tracy followed closely with a blender of homemade Baileys Irish Cream.

Rachael reached deep into the lapel pocket, extracted a crumbled piece of paper, cleared her throat, and began to read.

The great Chinese dragon which is the greatest dragon in all the world and which once upon a time was towed across the Pacific by a crew of coolies rowing in an open boat ...[†]

"The great Chinese dragon ... in an open boat ..."
Lawrence Ferlingetti: "The Great Chinese Dragon," *Starting from San Francisco,* New Directions Publishing Corp., 1967.

Trifecta

A food fight, adolescent males blowing off steam in the school cafeteria at the end of the semester: beans, greens, and cornbread flung against battleship-gray walls, catsup-soaked fish sticks airborne into the rafters, weaponized apples and bananas projected among socio-economic strata.

From his chair at the head of the jock table, Kyle Donovan slammed his cafeteria tray hard onto the Formica surface. His hot dog scooted across the floor, leaving a trail of yellow mustard in its wake. His coke bounced two feet in the air before splashing hard onto the floor. He swung his hand across the table, sending greasy French fries into his girlfriend's lap. "I can't believe it!"

With that he stomped out of the side door, darted across the parking lot to his father's Thunderbird, and screeched off in a cloud of burnt rubber.

I sat quietly at a table in the back of the cafeteria, waiting for my girlfriend Connie, our first opportunity to be together that day.

"What was that about?" I asked when she slid into the seat beside me.

"It's official, your sister Nancy, first in her class. She beat Kyle by a third of grade point after she aced her physics exam. There goes his trifecta down the drain."

"Trifecta?"

"Captain of the basketball team, president of the student council, and class valedictorian. His father has already scheduled a party at the country club."

Nancy's superlatives dominated our family's conversation over dinner that evening. Dad spoke first, "This calls for a celebration."

"I hear the ballroom at the country club is available," I offered.

My remark drew disapproving frowns. Undeterred, I tried again. "Connie says you'll give a speech at graduation."

"I'm working on it."

Mom leaned across the table and laid her hand on Nancy's. "Some advice for your classmates. That's the usual approach."

"I said I'm working on it."

"Perhaps something Eleanor Roosevelt may have said."

"Who? Like what?"

"I'm not sure, but I know she was a wise woman."

Dad bounded across the room and returned with the family copy of *Bartlett's Familiar Quotations.* "This one's always good advice," Mom said, leafing through the pages. "Learn from the mistakes of others. You can't live long enough to make them all yourself."

Nancy waved that one off. "Too preachy, too lame, maybe something a bit more stimulating, less dated."

Mom was undeterred. "Or this one? 'Do what you feel in your heart to be right. You'll be criticized anyway, damned if you do, and damned if you don't.'"

Dad offered his take. "That's my father's advice: 'Don't let the bastards get you down.'"

Mom retreated to her fallback. "Go with your heart."

"I'm working on it."

I agreed with Dad. "I'd go with 'Don't let the bastards get you down.'"

"I said I'm working on it."

"Have it your way," Mom said. "But I wish we'd had more notice. I'd have fixed something special for dinner."

"Meatloaf is fine."

Nancy was up all night, pecking away on her typewriter. There was a rhythm to the process: silence, then keys pounded in short spurts, paper ripped from the carriage, wadded, and lofted into the trash can, alternating groans and cheers.

Several times I heard her on the phone with a friend. "Is this trite? long-winded? mean-spirited? a cliché?"

Shortly after midnight she met me at the kitchen table where we shared the rest of the meatloaf. Totally out of character, she solicited my advice. She slipped a sheet of paper onto the table beside my plate. "I hate it when you offer your opinion, but for once I need someone to tell me the truth. Read this and tell me what you think."

The last sentence stood out because of the multiple erasure smears where she delved into a laundry list of bastards: cheerleaders, football players, assistant principals, 1950s' males, mothers of 1950s' males, racists, hypocrites, evangelists, rude automobile mechanics, and Kyle Donovan.

I began with a wishy-washy answer. "I don't know. What do you think?"

"I asked you first."

"A little raw for a graduation speech."

"Should I tone it down?"

"I don't know. What do you think?"

She shoved another paper in front of me. "How about this? Don't raise your daughters to be secretaries and cheerleaders."

"I've heard that before."

"When?"

"Once or twice from you."

"Nowhere else?"

"It's all yours."

Just before dawn she typed her final draft, a continuous forty-five-minute barrage, steady at the keys without a pause. She emerged from her room for breakfast with a neat stack of paper.

Mom spoke first, "Over easy or scrambled?"

"Scrambled."

Dad spoke next. "Well?"

"You won't like it."

"Might, might not, won't know until I hear it."

When her speech finally materialized on graduation day, Nancy delivered an impressive performance. She began with a smooth blend of seemingly contradictory personalities. "In the words of Eleanor Roosevelt: Do what you feel in your heart to be right—for you'll be criticized anyway. In my father's words: Don't let the bastards get you down."

Along the way she offered copious advice for those willing to listen: "Mothers, don't raise your sons to be 1950s' males. Fathers, don't raise your daughters to be sniveling appendages to 1950s' males. Girls, make your own way with your own brains. Boys, grow up, please. Assistant principals, consider some other line of work. Evangelists, knock on somebody else's door."

In addition to Dad and Eleanor Roosevelt, she quoted Dr. Seuss, "Be who you are and say what you mean because those who mind don't matter and those who matter don't mind"; Jane Austen, "If adventure will not befall a young lady in her own village, she must seek them abroad"; Carson McCullers, "If you would not be forgotten as soon as you are gone, either write things worth reading or do things worth writing"; and Edith Wharton, "If only we'd stop trying to be happy we'd have a pretty good time".

Near the end she spun off a list of individuals who had helped her along the way: "My mother for her patience. My future sister-in-law Connie James for saving my little brother Bill from himself. My kindergarten teacher Miss Cross for laying a foundation of curiosity and discovery. My girlfriends for unerring support and encouragement. My English teacher Mrs. Baker who taught me to write coherently. My Aunt Mary who kept me in touch with my feelings whether I could think of any at the moment or not. My grandmother for her Jane Austen quote."

Dad beamed throughout the speech after Nancy began with his bastard quotation. "After all, it's not often I'm mentioned in the same sentence as Eleanor Roosevelt."

In the reception after the speech, Kyle Donovan's mother personally complimented Nancy for her insight. "I may have erred with Kyle's socialization, but I'll do a better job with his two young brothers."

Over the years Nancy continually questioned her nineteen-year-old self with the same doubts: "too trite? too long-winded? too mean-spirited? a cliché?"

But if anyone wants my opinion, I'm thankful for my sister. Her nineteen-year-old world view has served me well. If she hadn't warned me about my inner 1950s' male, Connie might have left me along the way.

Green Card

Tuesday is huevos rancheros day at Software Solutions: whole-wheat tortillas, eggs over easy, goat cheese, guacamole, peppers, peach salsa, chorizo. The food is free, one of many perks for our elite cadre of software engineers. Our chef José Rodriguez ran the kitchen at La Casita Mexicana before we lured him away with more money and shorter hours. Our startup is a cosmopolitan firm, employing top talent from around the world. We treat our people well.

My second-floor corner office faces east over the river, as far as possible from the marketing people on the third floor and the executives on the fourth. Tuesdays midmorning, I slip down the rear stairway to the cafeteria for a late breakfast.

On July 21, 2020, just as I headed out the door, a notification from my boss popped up on my workstation console: "Can you handle Farid's Green Card renewal? I'm out of the office today."

I checked my watch, 9:30. The cafeteria served breakfast until 11:00. There was still time if I moved quickly. I settled back into my chair and begrudgingly clicked "accept" beside the scheduled meeting. I was conveniently in the office while my supervisor was conveniently out of the office.

Farid Akbar was twenty years my senior, having entered the computer field after three decades as a university professor in the Middle East. From the beginning I was destined for a well-paid but soulless career counting beans for corporate America. He is proud and structured. I'm roll-with-it unstructured, the boss's other-duties-as-assigned guy. He's a loner who hangs out in his cubicle surrounded by photographs of his family and homeland. I wander the halls with a clipboard of project plans, monitoring the workflow as projects proceed through the organization. I dine on prime rib with my buddies in the cafeteria. He lunches alone at his desk on stuffed grape leaves, kafta balls, and falafel.

10:00 a.m. Yet another cog in a meandering bureaucracy, my office, fifteen prescribed minutes. Farid stood before me, square-shouldered behind his PhD in Ancient Near Eastern Philosophy. He has a reputation here at the office, a chip on his shoulder, quite a few actually. He's tired of crap being thrown in his face.

But you have to understand, it's not our fault he no longer teaches Ancient Near Eastern Philosophy at a defunct Palestinian university. We're not in the philosophy business. We design statistical software for government economists, seven thousand miles and a couple thousand years from the Ancient Near East.

I said, "Hello Farid, have a seat."

He gave me his I've-heard-this-before look.

I continued, "Farid, I don't like this any more than you, but, fifteen minutes, that's the process. We endorse your Green Card. You work in your cubicle another year."

I hate it when I say process. He hates it when I say cubicle. I gave him my work-with-me-on-this look. He gave me his give-me-a-reason look. I shot back with my I've-got-problems-too look. He lapsed into his version of American colloquial. "Let's just do it, man."

"That's why we're here. Have a seat."

"I'm fine standing."

"Suit yourself."

"Is this where we access my moral character?"

I pulled the application from his folder. "That's one of the questions."

For the next fifteen minutes we struggled through paperwork. "Full name of father? Full name of mother? Do you have any children? How many? Ever in the military or police service? Educational qualifications? Sexual orientation? Religious affiliation?"

The tension in the room increased with each question. He stood before me unflinching. I squirmed around in my chair, chewing on my ballpoint and fingering my empty coffee cup.

"Have you visited any foreign country while staying in the United States?"

"Palestine."

"Your application says Israel."

"It used to be Palestine."

My disengaged left hemisphere submerged. Visions of goat cheese and guacamole appeared. Regrettably I lost my patience, "Farid, do you have a bug up your ass?"

Farid stiffened his shoulders, channeled the modern Near East, "I had the Israelis up my ass when I traveled back home for my grandmother's last rites, a small family cemetery on the West Bank tucked between a kibbutz and an army base, ten miles and four checkpoints from my landing strip."

Farid didn't appreciate processes, fifteen bureaucratic minutes, then we'd extend his Green Card another year. I reached for my pen to check "Forward Without Reservations" when our session spilled over into ancient turf wars.

We were so close to his Green Card, to my huevos rancheros. I could taste the chorizo. I could hear Jose's fork mashing avocados into guacamole.

Minute sixteen emerged. Farid shifted into overdrive, "The Israelis stuck a probe up my ass in case I was delivering a condom of contraband to dead terrorists who can't do any harm because they're dead."

"Dead?" I asked.

"Yes, my uncle and my brother."

I checked a few boxes, signed off on his paperwork. Twenty minutes later I sat in a booth in the cafeteria dousing double diablo hot sauce on my eggs. He returned to his cubicle for another year of bullshit. Another day, another checkpoint.

Rules for Repelling a Bear

In my father's defense, he didn't start it. The bear did. Our family moved to the hilltop years before our burly friend wandered down the Potomac River from Garrett County. When we bought the property, we had no inkling that we'd share the ridge with a brutish black beast, prowling the tree line, kicking over garbage cans, and terrorizing the neighborhood. We had no idea that forty miles up the North Branch a newborn bear cub cuddled with his momma deep in their den beneath the late spring snows.

The bear dominates my childhood memories. I was six, maybe seven, on a nondescript fall evening in the early 1950s. Dad and I surveyed the backlot, pruning his apple trees for the winter.

"Ice storms," he warned, moving from tree to tree, running his gloves along the branches. "Sleet and hail can demolish an orchard in fifteen minutes."

We went to bed that night a secure family. Throughout the night the kitchen dogs pranced in and out of our beds. The porch dogs groveled in the crawl space and clawed at the front door. My otherwise fearless sister Mary whimpered at my parent's bedside. "Rusty's scared. I think the bobcat is back."

Dad reassured her. "It's just a thunderstorm on the other side of the mountain."

"That's what you said when the bobcat ate your peacocks."

Mom piled on, "I don't buy this thunderstorm thing. Last night was a crisp fall evening."

I awoke that morning to the rumble of the barn doors along their rollers. For the first time in my life, I sensed fear in Dad's voice. He shouted from the backlot. "Sam! Get out here! You won't believe this."

I pulled up my jeans as I rounded the knoll onto the backlot. Dad, dressed in his beekeeper gear, sorted through the rubble, righting the overturned hives onto their cement block bases. He positioned another block on top of each hive box for ballast and stood back to judge the impact.

Clearly upset, he ran through the possibilities. "The wind wasn't so strong last night. It wasn't the bobcat. We'd have heard it. Or a mountain lion. The dogs would've gone crazy."

"We don't have mountain lions here," I reminded him.

"Be that as it may..." is as close as Dad got to admitting a mistake. He pulled the netting off his head as he spoke. "The bees are angry this morning. Something's riled them."

I followed him across the field to the fence where he discovered a swatch of black fur on a nail. He held it up in the morning light for a better look, then smelled it. The possibilities percolated. "Sam, looks like we have a bear problem."

Back in his workshop in the barn loft he slipped off his protective gear. "A salesman lives and dies by his Rolodex," he explained as he spun through the cards. "Dan Folk, Dan Folk, Dan Folk—Bingo!"

He wrenched the card from the wheel and waved it in the air. "This guy knows his bees."

"Who is Dan Folk?" I asked.

"Only the premiere beekeeper in western Maryland."

He turned his attention to his phone conversation. "Dan, I need your help...No, this isn't your shit-for-brains brother-in-law...Stuart Guthrie...Yes, that Stuart Guthrie...You know which Stuart this is...the one who put the fix in on your zoning citation...the one who got you a deal on a set of all-season radials...Can you stop by today? I have a problem with my bees, a big-assed bear problem...Great...Whenever it's convenient...I'll make it worth your while...I know my money's no good."

He dialed the next number from memory, Harold Beaufort, Garrett Tire's expert on tread and skid marks. "After all," he explained into the receiver. "A bear track isn't much different than a tire track. Forensics are forensics."

By mid-afternoon he'd assembled his team, some more qualified, some less so, but all enthusiastic. Each owed Dad. "I run the favor bank around here," he boasted. "I always maintain a healthy balance."

First to arrive was a squat man with a Masonite clipboard, a narrow tie, and a pocket protector, obviously Harold Beaufort.

Dan Folk was next on the scene with his nephew in tow. "Kevin teaches biology at Frostburg. He knows a thing or two about wildlife."

Dan and Harold bonded immediately. Throughout the afternoon Dad snooped over their shoulders as they discussed bear forensics. Harold ceremoniously mixed a polymer plaster concoction in the trunk of his Oldsmobile, then followed Dan through the back lot, filling each bear track with a plaster cast. Dad brought up the rear scrutinizing their work. Harold examined the cement blocks the bear had flung from the top of the beehives. He whipped out his slide rule to calculate the exact trajectory of the blocks from the beehives to the barn: how much force was required, where it hit, how fast it traveled, the depth of the dent in the siding.

"This is the exact same claw," Dan explained, nervously twisting his goatee. "The middle claw is misshapen, and the thumb is missing, definitely the same bear we identified in Garrett County last summer."

"The same bear?" Dad puzzled. "Which same bear as what where?"

Dan lowered his head to stare above his glasses, "The bear on your backlot last night was the same one that demolished Yoder's hives on Sang Run Creek."

Dad breathed silently and deeply. "The same bear? Sang Run Creek? That's forty miles upstream."

Dan stood his ground. "I'm not here to argue with you, but your man agrees it was the same bear. The middle claw was clearly crushed at some point."

Harold gestured with his slide rule to the plaster casts along the fence line. "The science points to Folk's bear."

"These Sang Run bears tend to be territorial," Dan warned. "Don't encroach on his territory."

"How do I know where his territory ends and mine begins? He wants everything: the barn, the garbage cans, my hives."

By the time we served our guests the traditional Sunday afternoon apples and popcorn and sent them down the hillside, Dad had a firm idea of our adversary. He tried the name aloud a few times. "Sang Run, Sang Run, I got you in my sights now."

The day ended with Dad rifling through the file cabinet for confirmation of our claim to the hilltop. "I don't think the bear recognizes the land records at the courthouse," Mom reminded him.

"I need to wrap my brain around this," Dad said, "Sang Run undoubtedly operates on an aboriginal territory system, something mystical, something spiritual."

"You're telling me that the Great Bear Spirit inadvertently bequeathed the same land to two parties? This is not an anthropomorphic bear."

Dad's position was firmly grounded in his Protestant work ethic. "I don't know where this bear gets off thinking he can share in the honey without doing any of the work. Did I see that bear lugging beehives up the hillside? No! Did I see the bear on the last Thursday of the month at the Frostburg Beekeepers meeting? No!"

The source of the honey was problematic. Before the apple orchard matured, the bees had only a patch of scrawny wildflowers along the highway. A few consultations with Mr. Folk established this was meadow honey. Dad was after sweet orchard honey. Not satisfied with his paltry output, he decided to prime the pump with a few jars from Yoder's Amish Market.

He made a big whoop-de-do, replete with bee netting and smokers as he pretended to retrieve several quarts of store-bought honey from each of his hives. The ruse worked too well. For Mary's 4-H project, she and Mom opened a stand at the Frostburg Farmers Market. Dad was called out of town on business before he could forestall the operation. For the first year in recent memory, a Yoder didn't win the best honey prize. Mom and Mary won a blue ribbon with pure Yoder's honey.

"Not a word of this," Dad warned me. "Only the two of us know we beat the Amish with their own honey. Let's leave it at that."

Dad was able to fool the 4-H judges and the Washington County Beekeepers Association with the source of the honey. He couldn't fool the bear who soon discovered the Yoder's stash in the barn, a cache that tempted him beyond his bear spirituality. A three-hundred pounder requires an ungodly calorie count to sustain his heft.

Dad's relationship with the bear was pure gamesmanship. There were rules and strategies. He was always aware of the score. He knew when he was winning and when the bear was winning. The bear only knew when he had honey in his belly. Mom also knew who was winning and who was losing. Her property was overrun. She was losing. "Maybe we should call animal control," she suggested over breakfast one morning.

"Not necessary. I know that bear. Give me a month or two to work out the details."

Mom was unconvinced. "Am I to accept it on faith that you have a three-hundred-pound beast in a gentleman's agreement not to eat any dogs or children?"

"There's no danger to the dogs. They're not interested in a fight."

"I know, they've moved into the crawl space."

"I have the situation under control," Dad insisted. "To catch a bear, you have to think like a bear."

"And precisely how do you think like a bear?"

"Dan Folk's nephew Kevin teaches biology at Frostburg. Maybe he can offer some pointers."

Although we seldom saw the bear, we heard him and witnessed his handiwork: markings on the trees, jostled hives. Dad made a mock beehive along the tree line and seeded it with corn syrup. The bear would have none of that. He went straight for our beehives with Yoder's honey.

"A rookie mistake," he admitted. "I got cheap with the corn syrup, should have used grocery store honey."

Dad was running out of sportsmanlike ideas. He stepped across the line one evening with a loathsome trick, a baited trap with a noose and a cowbell. When the bear took the bait, the cowbell tightened around his neck, ending his stealth for several months until the rope fabric wore thin.

Dad won one argument with Mom. "Our adventures with the bear will spill over into the boy's academic performance," he insisted.

Mom found such speculation ridiculous. Imagine her surprise when I brought home B-minus from Mrs. Franklin, my fifth-grade teacher. She found my depiction of man-vs-nature to be authentic, a true adventure with a wild animal. "I would have marked your paper a solid B except for your incessant digressions into booby traps, noise makers, and vials of bear pee."

Mom wasn't so enthused. "We're lucky she didn't call a social worker to report child endangerment."

On a typical morning, when the other children prepared for school in their suburban split-level kitchens, I sat in the bay window at our ranch house, slurping corn flakes, my eyes locked on the backlot for a glimpse of a black shape darting among the hives. None of my schoolmates had a beast in their yard. Not even the children of the most fearsome hill people had a father locked in mortal combat with a gargantuan black bear. I was the envy of elementary school, a young boy who believed in my father's infallibility.

My mother shared no such illusion. "That bear will ruin us."

When Dad was away on business, she was in charge, a totally a different ballgame. I awoke one morning to ungodly curses. Mom stood on the back stoop, firing my BB gun into the tree line.

"Mom," I advised her, "the bear doesn't know the difference between a BB and a bee sting. You need something bigger."

"What do you suggest?"

Mary provided the solution. "Dad keeps a shotgun in the umbrella rack in the mudroom and buckshot shells on the top shelf of the pantry."

The next morning gunshots rang across the property. Mom crouched on the back stoop, firing into the tree line. Mary stood at her side, shoving cartridges into the breech when Mom reloaded. Mom braced the gunstock against the doorjamb to absorb the recoil. Each blast sent shockwave through the house. Flower vases teetered and fell from the mantel. I retreated to the corner, cringing for the poor bear. Mom stood her ground, fire in her eyes, curses dancing on her tongue. "Come out in the open, you son-of-a-bitch. I dare you."

As Mary remembered it years later. "Mom let loose a decade of pent up 1950s' housewife aggression on that poor unfortunate creature."

The bear soon learned to distinguish between Dad, an adversary who played by the rules, and Mom, who didn't. In her defense, the rules weren't written down anywhere. Unfortunately for our burly friend, Dad was away on business most of the summer at a series of automotive shows in the Midwest. In his absence Mom stood guard on the back stoop, ready to fire into the darkness at any sound or movement. The poor bear faced a dwindling supply of honey guarded with cold, hard steel. Any other creature would have thrown in the towel and wandered off. But this was our nemesis bear with an acute sense of smell. He was keenly aware of Dad's stash of Amish honey in the barn.

I woke up one morning to Mom's shrill war-hoop. "I got you out in the open like the stupid bear you are."

I rushed to the kitchen window in time to see our bear, honey dripping from his jowls, in a rapid retreat toward the tree line. "Why'd you do that?" he mumbled in bear whimpers as he scampered off. His self-respect fizzled.

Mom's spirit soared. "That felt good."

She flipped open the breech of her shotgun, emptied the remaining shells onto the kitchen floor, and stuffed the shotgun into the umbrella rack, just like in the movies. Pumped with adrenaline, she grabbed me by the collar and pinned me against the refrigerator. "Not a word to your father about this."

"Not a word," I submitted.

"That goes for you too," she snarled at Mary.

After Mom left the room, I retrieved one of the remaining shells from the floor and showed it to Mary. "Look at this. Mom's last barrage was slugs, not buckshot. Where did these come from?"

"I found them Dad's toolbox after we went through the shells in the pantry."

Dad returned from his automotive expos flush with cash, strutting, ready to resume combat. "I don't understand," he said on our morning stroll onto the backlot.

"Understand what?" I asked.

"The bullet holes in the barn door. I've never noticed them before."

"Oh that!"

He eyed me as if I might know something he didn't. "When was the last time you saw that bear?"

I knew the exact moment. It was etched in my brain, then slammed up against the refrigerator. I answered as best I could. "I don't remember. Wait. Now that I think about it, I heard him growl late one night, sort of a good-bye growl."

"Never mind," Dad said, turning his attention to the hillside. "Let's have a look over the ridge, see what we can see."

We didn't find anything.

A week later Dan Folk stopped by the house for a visit. "Thought you might want to know your bear was spotted in high Garrett County, raiding the Yoder's beehives."

"You sure it's the same bear?" Dad asked.

"There's another toe missing, but the other tracks are identical, took us awhile to make a positive ID. Your man Beaufort still had the casts in his warehouse. Looks like your bear problems are over."

We never saw the bear again. There never was a final battle. Without an adversary Dad lost interest in the backlot and his bees. Soon thereafter he was promoted to Vice President for Marketing at Garrett Tire. He no longer needed a bear to stoke his ego or his imagination.

Mom never turned violent again, but the day she blew off the bear's toe, she came into her own. Mary thrived as well. She emerged from her study alcove more than an academic machine.

She shared Mom's awakening. Their world was no longer centered around the kitchen table and Girl Scout projects.

As for me, I was left behind, struggling between two parental bookends, two conflicting loyalties, one to my father, one to my mother, two coerced oaths:

> *Not a word to your mother about my secret honey source, better she doesn't know.*

> *Not a word to your father about the shotgun, better he doesn't know.*

About the Author

George Miller has lived most of his life in Maryland, from his childhood in the mountain town of Cumberland to his retirement outside North Beach on the western shore of the Chesapeake Bay. Along the way he has been a motorcycle messenger, an army officer during the Vietnam War, a single father, an economist, a computer programmer, an environmentalist, and a writer.

He holds degrees from Davidson College, the University of North Carolina, and American University.

He is the author of several works, including *The Best Free Verse Ten Dollars Can Buy* (a book of poems) and *Cooper Finds Her Thermal* (an illustrated allegory about a Cooper's Hawk who sets out to save the Chesapeake Bay (www.cooperfindsherthermal.com).

His work has appeared in *American Writers Review*, Calvert County Library's *Southern Maryland Art and Poetry: celebrating our waterways, UpStart* (Annapolis Art District Magazine), and *Liminal Spaces, A Collection of Poetry and Poetry-infused Art* (a publication of the Arts Lab of South County). His poem "Flat Bottoms, God Bless'em" won first prize in the 2022 New Bay Books Inaugural Writers on the Water competition.

Miller has also published books under several labels for fellow southern Maryland authors.

As his eighth decade approaches, he plans to continue writing as long as he is able, and his readers are receptive. He is thankful to all who have supported him.

www.ingramcontent.com/pod-product-compliance
Lightning Source LLC
Chambersburg PA
CBHW040909010826

48978CB00013BB/1212